JANE AUSTEN INVESTIGATES

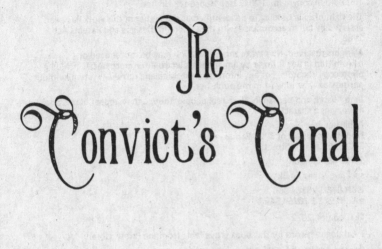

The Convict's Canal

Julia Golding

LION FICTION

Published by
Lion Hudson, Part of SPCK Group
SPCK, 36 Causton Street,

SW1P 4ST London

spckpublishing.co.uk

ISBN 978 1 78264 366 1
e-ISBN 978 1 78264 346 3

First edition 2022

A catalogue record for this book is available from the British Library

Printed and bound in the UK, October 2022, LH26

Editor's Note

Notebooks containing details of Jane Austen's first investigations were recently found hidden in a trunk stored in the attics of Jane's family home. There are signs that Jane expected her papers to be discovered, for they begin with a warning from young Jane herself.

Warning

Any resemblance to persons living or dead in these case notes is entirely intentional. Names of people and places have been changed to protect the wicked – but you know who you are!

J.A.

Chapter 1

1789

"Henry has invited us to Oxford at last!" declared Cassandra, waving a letter high in the air as she raced across the rectory lawn.

Jane looked out from the apple tree. She was perched on a lower branch, hand encircling the nearest fruit. She had just been thinking that the russet's grey-green skin was not very promising in appearance, but looks could be deceptive: the flesh was delicious.

"Did you hear me?" called Cassandra.

Jane picked the apple and put it in her basket. She held on to a branch and leaned out of the tree. "I think the inhabitants of the Shetland Islands heard you."

Cassandra put her hands on her hips. "Oh you! The neighbours perhaps, but no one outside Steventon."

The sisters grinned at each other, Jane enjoying her vantage point, Cassandra happy on the ground. Jane's perch felt like a crow's nest in the good ship *Apple Tree* and her sister an island in the grassy sea. Time for Jane to go ashore.

"Why has Henry invited us now?" Jane passed down the basket. "I thought our esteemed elder brother did not want his sisters anywhere near his university friends?" Henry had teased Jane that she and Cassandra would destroy what little reputation he had among the students of Oxford's colleges: Cassandra would instantly be declared Henry's superior in looks, Jane in intelligence. Thank goodness St John's College did not take women, he had said, or he would exist completely in their shade.

"He has relented." Cassandra held the ladder steady so Jane could descend in a ladylike fashion. Jane instead jumped down from her branch with only minor damage to her petticoat. She snatched the letter from Cassandra. Henry's letters were always very amusing, upholding the Austen tradition that no chance for a good joke should be missed.

My dear Cassandra (and troublesome Jane)...

"Troublesome?" Jane pointed at the salutation. "If he thinks that's an insult, he'll have to try harder!"

"I think he rather believes it a compliment." Cassandra selected a russet from Jane's basket, finding one without wormholes or pecks from venturesome birds.

"Humph to that!"

The fellows at my college have implored me to rescind my ban on entertaining any female Austens in Oxford during my sojourn here at the university. Poor fools, they do not understand the danger. I was trying to keep them safe. To be trounced by a fledgling of thirteen would be a salutary lesson, so I have decided they must be taught this by experience.

Therefore, with the permission of our honoured parents, I duly invite you to visit me next week. Some of the colleges are getting together to pit their best men against each other on the river and I thought you might find it highly amusing. I have been chosen for my college boat in the VERY IMPORTANT position of stroke.

Do come.

Yrs. Affectionately,

Henry

That was the real reason for the invitation, realized Jane: Henry wanted their support.

"Good gracious! They'll sink for certain!" she said, already imagining the scene of the boat heading directly into the bank at top speed (her brother was not known for his level-headedness).

"But we must go nonetheless." Cassandra started up the slope to the rectory, carrying the basket, lifting her dress out of the way of the long grass.

Jane tramped behind, reconciled to her muddy hem. "Of course we must. If he goes down, he goes down in glorious style to the applause of his relatives, as any Austen would."

"Quite so." The two girls sniggered, of one mind on the subject. It was highly unlikely Henry would survive the week without at least one dousing in the Thames. That was worth the price of the coach ticket all by itself.

Their mother, however, was less impressed by the invitation.

"I do not think it appropriate for you two to be gadding off again. I spared you to go to the ball in Reading, so I am not inclined to think it is time so soon for another party of pleasure." She weighed the sugar carefully on the scales then tipped it into a big pan, where it joined the bubbling fruit.

"You will recall, Mama, that I did not want to go to Reading," Jane slipped in. Her mother ignored her, as usual, her attention on her elder daughter.

"There is so much bottling to do, and no one makes jam quite as well as you, Cassandra. When I gave the jars to our neighbours last Christmas, your raspberry was declared a triumph by the Biggses." Mrs Austen's strong nose dominated her face much as her strong opinions ruled the rectory, overwhelming any cheek. Jane always felt her own little narrow nose a disappointment, somehow a symbol of her unimportance in the world. She sneaked a blackberry from the pile waiting to go into the pan. She was never going to turn the head of a worthy suitor, say someone with five thousand a year and his own library. Cassandra might when she was fully out in society. Jane would have to hope she would be allowed to visit her future married sister and consult the collection.

"I can stay up all night making the jam, Mama," said Cassandra. "I really think I can get it all done and still be in time for the river races."

"I'll help!" volunteered Jane.

"No!" said Cassandra, at the same time as her mother said:

"That will not be necessary."

Jane had spoiled the last batch, letting it burn when she got caught up in a riveting chapter in the latest novel she had borrowed from the circulating library. What was plum jam compared to an elopement and threat of dire disgrace for the heroine?

Her father came into the kitchen, Jane's dog, Grandison, trotting at his heels. They had just been for a ramble around the parish. Mr Austen went to visit his flock of churchgoers, Grandison to receive the pats and strokes he thought his due when Cassandra and Jane had been too busy to pamper him.

"What's this, my dear?" Mr Austen's dark eyes twinkled with intelligence under his white wig. He was a strongly built man, though by no means tall, equally used to working on his farm, teaching in school, and preaching in church. Jane thought him quite the perfect gentleman with no false airs or pretensions.

"Henry has inconsiderately invited the girls to Oxford – but I can't possibly spare them." Mrs Austen ushered Grandison out to the yard, having discerned that the dog's paws were muddy. Jane got a rag out of the bag and wet it under the pump. She would let Cassandra fight this battle, as her sister was her mother's favourite. Jane rather hoped she might be her father's, but he was careful to show equal love to all his children.

"It won't be long until winter sets in and the roads will be too bad for them to travel far," observed Mr Austen, taking the armchair by the kitchen fire. Cassandra offered him a russet, which he took with a nod of thanks. He rubbed it on his waistcoat.

"Girls should be kept at home – out of trouble." Mrs Austen poured him a cup of tea.

Jane could have pointed out that her mother had found it convenient to hold a very different opinion when she sent Jane off to Southmoor Abbey and to her old school in Reading, both but a few months ago. Yet she held her tongue and waited. Grandison submitted to having his paws wiped, even licking her cheek in return. He always approached the world as if it were destined to provide the black-and-white crossbreed with nothing but good things – cuddles, treats, things to chase. He was usually right.

It was a shame that second daughters weren't so universally welcomed.

"I see your point, Mrs Austen," her father said peaceably. "Indeed, I do. Might there be any of that cake from yesterday remaining?"

Mrs Austen fetched him a slice, bestowing also a pleased smile at his deferral to her judgment. "Here you are, my dear."

"Much obliged. However, on the subject of Oxford…"

Jane readied herself for the next words he said. Something in the atmosphere told her things were going to change in the same way the barometer falling heralded rain.

"… I had thought to go back to the old place myself, enjoy a short respite from my labours and consult my colleagues. I would welcome the girls to accompany me and run my errands."

Put like that, with both Jane and Cassandra being "useful" – Mrs Austen's most prized quality for young ladies – it would be difficult for their mother to object.

Mrs Austen frowned, like a housewife suspecting the grocer had put bruised fruit at the bottom of the basket. "But what about all the work there is to do here?"

Mr Austen swallowed a mouthful of ginger cake. "Oh, there must be far less when I'm not around. You always say I create a lot of fuss and bother with all my comings and goings. And I'll send my pupils away to help Farmer Bates with his harvest; they'll appreciate the change too. You can have the house to yourself and enjoy a holiday."

Mrs Austen's face softened. She was clearly already imagining the luxury of sitting in her parlour without having to jump up and solve one or more domestic crises every hour.

"If you think it a good idea…?"

"I think it the very best of ideas," Mr Austen said firmly. "All that remains is to warn Henry to arrange lodgings for the three of us."

Chapter 2

Travelling with their father, Jane discovered, was a far more comfortable affair than taking the stagecoach. He hired a private carriage, and they had it completely to themselves, changing horses where and when they wished, not bound by any timetable. This meant they could stop when they wanted and make a holiday of the journey. Indeed, they did break the trip at the bustling towns of Newbury and Abingdon, mainly, Jane suspected, so her father could visit the local clergymen.

"Have you noticed," Jane said to Cassandra as they waited in the carriage outside a pretty vicarage with a doorway surrounded by yellow roses, "that Papa has better access to information throughout the kingdom than the government?"

Cassandra looked up from the silk purse she was sewing as a Christmas gift. "That is true now you mention it."

"If ever we should find ourselves at war and fearing the enemy among us, they should ask him to keep an eye on what is going on." Jane rested her head on her palm, elbows propped on her knees. It wasn't a ladylike pose, but another benefit of private travel was that there was no one to see.

Cassandra embroidered the sails of her needlework ship with white satin-stitch. "Do you think there will be a war?"

"Papa is worried there will be. He thinks the French have gone quite mad, pulling down their prisons and declaring everyone equal. He's most concerned for our cousin." Their cousin Eliza had married the Comte de Feuillide and had a little boy called Hastings. She seemed an immensely romantic figure to Jane – having married into French nobility and living in a faraway land. Such heroines were always destined for a horrible time in novels, a prospect that made Jane anxious. Far safer, she reflected, to live an uneventful life in Hampshire.

Cassandra put aside her embroidery. "And do you think he's right to be worried?"

Jane shrugged. "How can we know, when even the great men are debating in Parliament if the French Revolution will turn out to be a good or a bad thing?"

Cassandra's lips quirked in a teasing smile. "But you always have an opinion – even when you don't have any facts."

Jane decided her sister deserved a tickling for that comment, so they were still tussling with each other and had reached the stage of weeping with laughter when their father came back. Grandison was again acting as his lieutenant, head cocked to receive his commands. Grandison barked to see the fun, but Mr Austen just clicked his tongue, said a weary "Enough, girls", and retook his seat.

Their father was so good-tempered. If it had been their mother on this journey, they would both now be walking the rest of the way, thought Jane, brushing her skirts straight.

Their route took them into Oxford over Friar Bacon's Bridge and up St Aldates, a street that climbed quite steeply between church and college buildings. Jane was excited to get her first glimpse of the university through the archway under a domed turret. The huge grass quadrangle beyond was strangely barren of ornament – no fountains, no statues, as if it had been rendered mute and plain by awareness of the clever fellows who surrounded it in their lodgings.

"That is Christchurch," her father said, seeing where her attention was directed, "fearful rival of the family college St John's. If Henry is rowing against them in his race, you can expect feelings to run high. There may be even some pushing into the river and widespread splashing." He waggled his brows, delighted by the prospect.

"That would be splendid," Jane agreed. She was never that bothered about winning games, but she did like to see them played with the right bloodthirsty spirit. No game of chase in the Austen household took place without someone getting tackled to the ground, Jane included, though Cassandra cried off these days, having reached the heady age of sixteen and more mindful of her frocks than fun.

"Why does it look like a fort?" Cassandra asked, noticing the formidable walls that prevented entry, apart from through the guarded gateways.

"Most of the colleges are like that," Mr Austen explained, "St John's even more so as the entrance looks like the gate to a castle. I was told that it stemmed from the Town and Gown Riots of 1355."

Jane snorted. "You would've thought they would've made up by now, ready to let down the drawbridge!"

Mr Austen shook his head sadly. "No, Jane, it is no laughing matter. Thirty local people died and over sixty students."

"Good heavens, what were they fighting about?" asked Cassandra.

Mr Austen sighed at the absurdity of mankind. "Two students complained about the wine at the Swindlebrook Tavern."

Jane gasped. "Just that? You aren't joking?"

He fixed the girls with a sharp look, always ready with his moral application (he couldn't help it because he was on the hunt for sermon material every week). "It just goes to show how small slights can bear evil fruit, my dears. There were seething tensions before the unfortunate students made their complaint, but this was the spark that exploded the gunpowder keg."

Jane looked at the fortified colleges with new eyes. No wonder the students liked keeping themselves tucked away in their grassy quads if the locals were apt to set upon them if they ventured beyond the walls.

They rattled along Cornmarket through the people going about their shopping. Jane inspected the men for any sign of hostility, but it seemed that for at least the moment the events of 1355 weren't uppermost in their minds. Of more interest today was the quality of the poultry hanging outside the butcher's and the bread stacked on the baker's counter. Housewives haggled with barrowmen; drinkers lounged outside the tavern; carters shouted to loitering students to clear a path through the narrow street. The roadway widened and the carriage then drew up outside St John's, the gateway impressively fortified as her father had promised.

"We're here!" declared Mr Austen.

Chapter 3

Jane's father jumped down with the eagerness of a younger man. Jane wondered if he was recalling his time as a student here forty years ago. He had stayed on to become a fellow of the college, before marriage and ordination took him away to life as a parish priest. Did he miss that bachelor life of study and quiet contemplation? He had swapped it for a wife, eight children, and numerous parishioners. From his happy smile as he looked up at the building, she thought it probable that there were a few pangs of regret about the path in life he had chosen. Still, she liked to think that his family brought him even more contentment, and he did appear to relish his role as their father.

She slid her arm through his.

"Do you miss it, Papa?"

Grandison sniffed at the base of a tree and added his own welcome. Jane hoped no one spotted him.

Mr Austen patted her hand. "It is very fine, is it not?"

"Indeed, it is."

"You would love the library."

"I imagine I would."

17

"Let's see if Henry has remembered that we are coming today." Offering his other arm to Cassandra, he led them into the porter's lodge.

They entered a dark room with slot windows just under the gateway. A mahogany desk separated visitors from the rows of pigeonholes behind. These were alphabetically arranged for each member of the college, and stuffed with letters and newspapers. A row of keys hung on pegs, meticulously labelled in a spidery handwriting. *Old Tower*, Jane spotted. *Library*. *Staircase 3*.

"Mr Austen!" crowed the elderly man at the desk. He was dressed in a dark suit and had but the merest froth of white hair surrounding his bald pate, reminding Jane of a magpie. "Or should I say, Reverend Austen? Who would've thought, eh?"

"Richards, I'm delighted to see you still here," her father declared with matching warmth.

"Why? Did you expect to see me in the churchyard then?" Laughter lines deepened. The porter rang a bell to summon an underling.

"Indeed, no. Merely enjoying your retirement from active service at the college."

"The day I don't work is the day they carry me out of my house feet first."

"A very fine sentiment." Mr Austen nodded to his daughters. "These are my girls: Miss Austen and Miss Jane Austen."

"Ah yes, your Henry said to expect them. We've arranged rooms for them with a landlady across the road. No ladies in college," he explained when he saw Jane's disappointment.

A boy came in, face flushed from running across the college in answer to the summons. He had pink cheeks and a shock of blond curls, and looked to be about Jane's age.

"Benjamin, take a message to Mr Austen that his family have arrived," said the porter.

The boy tugged his forelock and ran off.

"That's my grandson. Training him up to take over from my son when my son takes over from me."

Mr Austen always had the right words for such encounters. "Very fitting. It would be hard to imagine St John's without a Richards at the gate."

"Heaven gets St Peter; St John's gets a Richards," agreed the porter, perhaps rather overestimating the importance of his role if he was comparing himself with the greatest of the disciples. Still, Jane took it as a sign of how serious he was about his duties.

"How is the old place?" Mr Austen sat down on a bench to gossip. Jane and Cassandra took their seats demurely beside him, Grandison flopped at their feet. Jane imagined that anyone glimpsing the Austen sisters would believe they were the pattern cards of good behaviour – first impressions could be misleading.

"Same as ever, sir. Oxford, though, is sadly changed." The porter handed a key to a student who hurried through carrying a stack of books, the exchange happening with barely a slackening of pace.

"I never thought to hear that." Mr Austen nodded affably to a teaching fellow as he flitted through in his black cloak.

"Oh, but it is, sir." The happy expression slid from the porter's face like a pile of books tumbling from an overburdened shelf.

"How so?" Mr Austen tapped his forefinger on his folded hands.

"It's that dratted canal. They've dug up the meadows at the back of Worcester College and are building a big water basin just by the castle to take all the canal boats. What's a lake doing in the middle of Oxford, I ask you? This canal mania has gone too far. It was all right when it was a few fields they dug up, near the coal mines up north, but down here? An ugly scar, that's what it is, on the face of a beauty."

Mr Austen nodded in that peace-making way of his. Jane had actually heard him praise the canal-building Duke of Bridgwater and subsequent enterprising gentlemen who had criss-crossed the country with these water roads. Travel had never been so fast and so smooth for goods; the country was booming, according to her father.

"Still, Richards, doubtless you'll be happy to have your coal much cheaper come winter."

Richards scowled. "That's how they won the city fathers over: cheap coal! What's wrong with shivering a little?"

Her father must have concluded, as Jane had, that the man was not to be reasoned out of his opposition to this change. He let the matter drop. Some people just liked standing against new things, even if it brought them benefits.

"Papa!" Henry bounded into the lodge with energy to match Grandison's at his most exuberant. "And you brought the horrors with you!"

"That's no way to greet your sisters, sir," said Richards, but he was smiling again.

"You knew whom I meant though, did you not, Richards? I rest my case." Henry scooped Jane and Cassandra into a hug. "Now the fun can begin!"

"Begin?" queried their father. "I was under the impression it never ceased where you were concerned."

Chapter 4

Henry was an enthusiastic host. He gave Cassandra and Jane a quick tour of his college, throwing out such remarks as:

"The college library – not sure what's in there." This was said with a twinkle in his eye.

Or,

"Chapel – they wouldn't let me into the choir. Apparently, unlike at home, you have to be able to sing."

Mr Austen chuckled at that.

And,

"Hall – food is excellent. Don't tell Mama, but the cook's shepherd's pie is better than hers."

Everyone promised not to betray him. Mrs Austen prided herself on her local reputation as serving the best pie in England.

Their father followed a few steps behind, hands clasped behind his back. Jane could tell he was walking the paths of memory as surely as he trod the paving stones of his old college.

It was funny to think of her father as a young man here. Jane admired the pale yellow stone frontages, some with colonnades where students could walk on wet days and discuss high matters of learning – or, as Henry claimed, race tortoises and play battledore. The quadrangles were edged by the rooms where the St John men lodged, arranged on staircases like hats on a hatstand. Henry paused outside the entrance to his staircase, pointing to the signboard that listed the scholars who lived in rooms leading off the stairs. His name was near the top: *H. Austen*. Underneath were his friends, all fine fellows, he swore, as well as the most important occupant of this particular staircase, Dr J. Merryman. This gentleman lodged on the ground floor and was the owner of some fine flower-filled window boxes. He was the academic charged with attempting to stuff a little knowledge of the classics between Henry's ears.

Jane smiled at her brother's blithe remarks about the life of learning he was enjoying, but she couldn't suppress the deep longing that the sights woke inside her. What a chance Henry had! If only she could have a room to share with a clever companion, libraries to consult, lectures to attend, be free to come and go with no expectation that you should first finish the mending or pick the apples! And what an honour to live in a place that looked like a castle from one of her favourite gothic novels, doubtless full of intrigue and history! Henry was making light of his achievements, but he was a better scholar than he let on, genuinely interested in learning. He was downplaying his excitement to study here, probably because their father outstripped them all with his depth of knowledge; but Jane could tell that Henry was absorbing so much from his time in Oxford, making himself ready to face almost any challenge life would bring to him. When he graduated, he could look another man in the eye and know he likely knew as much as, if not more than, they did.

And what about the state of my brain? wondered Jane. *I have a patchwork education, patched and darned like the contents of the ragbag.* Henry was kind to play up her wit, but she knew she was lacking the breadth and depth that these scholars had. Her brothers were so fortunate. She would always feel… lesser, confined to the small and the local.

A line from one of her favourite poets came to her:

> Full many a flower is born to blush unseen,
> And waste its sweetness on the desert air.

That's me, she thought with a rare dose of self-pity, *unseen*.

A young man bolted around the corner and collided with her. Newton's laws of motion prevailed, and she went flying to the ground.

That's what I get for feeling sorry for myself, she thought wryly. *A wake-up call!*

"Oh my word! A thousand apologies!" The human cannonball helped her to her feet. Jane realized that her party had abandoned her. While she had been thinking melancholy thoughts, they had ascended to the heights of Henry's room, leaving her at the bottom of the staircase. "Did I damage you?" he asked.

Jane nursed a scraped palm but hid it in her skirts. An Austen didn't fuss about trifles. "Please, think nothing of it, sir."

"Nothing of it! I flattened you like the charge of Macedonian cavalry in the skirmishes of Alexander the

Great; or, more like one of Hannibal's elephants, taking on the Roman army."

Jane had time to take in the unfortunate charger as he muttered his classical self-condemnations. A freckle-faced young man with bright copper hair, tightly curled, he sparked with intelligence. She spotted a pair of spectacles in his breast pocket, rather than on his nose, which might explain his blundering into her.

"I accept the last comparison," she said. "I prefer to be the Romans who eventually prevailed over Hannibal, rather than the flattened victims of Alexander, no matter how great History judges him."

His mouth dropped open. "Good gracious, you must be Austen's sister! I heard you were coming today."

She bobbed a curtsey.

"Let me guess…" He donned the spectacles. "Miss Jane, the younger?"

"Indeed. What gave me away?"

His face flushed a little at that.

"He said I was the plainer sister and too clever for my own good?" guessed Jane, crossing her arms.

Henry hurried out of the staircase. He was the tallest and most handsome of the Austen brothers, with smiling dark eyes. "I never said you were plain, Jane." He winced at the rhyme. "I merely said Cassandra was the family belle and you the wit." Henry took stock of the circumstances in which he found his sister, sharp gaze catching the scrape on her hand. "I see you met my friend, Colin Jenkinson. Jenkinson, may I make my sister known to you?"

Jenkinson bowed. "It is an honour, Miss Jane."

"Now you've bowled her over like a ninepin, come upstairs

and see if you can knock over any more of my nearest and dearest. Jane, let me get you some water to wash that little hand."

If Jenkinson could have grown any redder, he would have been entirely scarlet. He followed Henry and Jane up the stairs.

"She said she was unhurt." His tone begged for Henry's understanding.

"An Austen doesn't fuss over trifles," Jane and Henry said in unison, then grinned at each other.

"Good gracious, a female edition of Henry Austen: the college won't survive," Jenkinson muttered so they both could hear.

"There are two more in our rooms," warned Henry. "Another female imprint and the original text, otherwise known as our Reverend Papa."

"The Lord preserve us from all perils and dangers of this night!" muttered Jenkinson, quoting from the Prayer Book.

Jane decided she liked Jenkinson.

Henry performed the introductions without any more of Jane's family ending up on the floor. Jane meanwhile bathed her hand. In addition to the scrape, she had jarred her wrist. The right one. She rotated it carefully, hoping the pain would quickly subside. It would make it difficult to hold a pen, but that would not stop her writing. She'd use her left if needs be. Being deprived of her quill was akin to clipping the wings of a bird.

She listened to what Henry was telling her father.

"Jenkinson is quite the cleverest among us. Start a line of Homer, and he'll finish it for you. Venture to cite Pliny, he'll not only correct you to whether it is the elder or the younger, but also mention the letter in which your half-remembered reference is to be found." Henry cut them all a slice from the seed cake he had set out ready to entertain his guests, clearly enjoying the uncommon experience of playing host to his family. He passed the first slice to Cassandra, prompting the realization in Jane that, without their mother present, her older sister was indeed the senior lady in the room and was to be treated as such. Cassie was growing up too fast for Jane's liking.

"Are you destined for the church, Mr Jenkinson?" asked Mr Austen. He was always on the lookout for clever curates for the churches of Hampshire.

Like any good spymaster would, thought Jane, taking her plate of cake from Henry. *Put good men in all the key positions.* She let the little fantasy run through her mind that her father was the mastermind of all the secret intelligence of the kingdom.

"No, sir. I believe my family would like me to take over the family business," Jenkinson said, not quite able to disguise his grimace at that prospect.

"Which is?" Mr Austen added a lump of sugar to his tea.

"Coal. We have a mine near Derby."

"Ah yes. I understand that many landowners have made their fortunes with coal. They earn thousands a year from these ventures. The new nobility – no titles but twice as rich." Mr Austen stirred his tea and tapped the rim of his cup with the teaspoon. "I suppose you welcome the canals? Your family must benefit from them?"

Jenkinson's brow furrowed. "You know, sir, I do believe I should have something very clever to say in response, but I am much happier discussing the exploits of ancient Odysseus than thinking of something witty about the price of coal."

"I doubt anyone could say anything witty about that," murmured Jane.

He bowed. "Thank you, Miss Jane."

"Come now, Jenks," said Henry, "it really is fascinating stuff, the way the country is changing!" Henry had always been the one who took an interest in business. "I find it very romantic: the silent, smooth gliding of tonnes of coal, passing through fields on water roads where beforehand they would have rattled and banged on the back of the cart. The canal system is our era's greatest contribution to the landscape. The medieval people left churches and castles; we are leaving waterways and water-powered factories."

"From that, one might conclude they worshipped God and we Mammon," quipped their father, "as we have chosen to build a very different kind of temple."

"My father has invested heavily but I can't see anything beautiful in a canal," said Jenkinson. "But what do the Miss Austens think?"

Cassandra glanced at Jane. "I have to admit I don't believe we've ever seen one up close."

Henry got to his feet. "We must remedy that immediately because there is one being built but a stone's throw from here."

"If you can throw a stone a quarter of a mile," said Jenkinson. "I know I can't."

Mr Austen was well used to his son's ways. "Henry, do take your seat. The canal isn't going anywhere. We can go tomorrow. Let your sisters find their lodgings first."

Henry did as bidden. "I say, you'll come with us, won't you, Jenks? I'd like to change your mind if I can."

Jenkinson smiled. "I doubt if you would change my mind, but how can I resist with the promise of such company?"

"Bravo, Jenks!" Henry clapped. "I do believe that is the first compliment to the fairer sex I have ever heard you make. That study you've put into the art has not been wasted."

Poor Jenkinson returned to his scarlet colouring.

"Whereas I see you have completely neglected the lesson as to when not to blurt out the first thing you are thinking," said their father reprovingly. "Mr Jenkinson will dare venture no more if you react in such an asinine manner."

"It was a very pretty compliment," said Cassandra, worried for Henry's friend. "Well done."

Finding the idea of composing compliments delightfully absurd, Jane chewed her cake vigorously to stop herself giggling and doing further damage to the young man's confidence. Her expectations of their Oxford adventure as being highly entertaining were well on their way to being fulfilled.

Chapter 5

As a former fellow of the college, their father was to roost within the walls; female Austens had to be content with a perch just outside St John's. Grandison was also to remain behind with the menfolk on the grounds that he was an honorary fellow (and Henry wouldn't part with him after a long absence from home). Jane had been reluctant to make that sacrifice, but her older brother had begged quite handsomely, telling her – Cassandra as witness – how Jane was absolutely the favourite of his sisters, at least for that day, so she felt it incumbent on her to be generous – at least for that day too.

Besides, Grandison would prefer the gardens of the college to the confines of the girls' bedroom, Jane had to admit.

With the assistance of the porter's grandson, the girls crossed the wide road of St Giles, the main thoroughfare north from the city centre, to arrive at their boarding house. Their luggage had already been sent ahead. The lodging house was tall and thin, squashed between other more substantial dwellings, like a timid man crammed in the middle bench at the theatre, shoulders pushed up to his ears, while rowdier fellows lounged around him.

The knock on the door was answered by a pleasingly appropriate personage in the beanpole of a landlady. Like a pot plant restricted by the depth of soil, she had grown to fit her house. Her dark hair was streaked with cobwebs of white. Jane was happy to see her apron was white, dress neat, and nails short and clean. *Never stay where the people carry dirt on themselves, as their beds will be no better*, her mother always warned.

"Mrs Hill, here are the young ladies," Benjamin the porter's boy announced, before tugging on his forelock and racing across the road, weaving through the carrier carts and mail coaches without hesitation.

"That boy!" said Mrs Hill, clucking her tongue. "Only one pace – a full canter." She looked them over and smiled. "Welcome, my dears. I hope you don't mind: I've put you in the topmost room. My other guests can't manage all the stairs. Old bones."

"Not at all," said Cassandra. "Thank you for letting us stay. I'm Cassandra and this is my sister, Jane."

"Pleased to meet you both. Jane – what a lovely straightforward name – and Cassandra, so… so fancy."

Jane grinned, understanding from the tone that for once her name was the preferred one of the two. So often it was dismissed as being too ordinary.

"Do you know the classics?" Jane asked as they followed in Mrs Hill's wake.

"Me, dear?" The lady laughed at the notion. "Indeed no, but you can't help picking up a thing or two with university guests staying with you."

Another female who had to cadge her education from what others let slip, Jane concluded.

"Cassandra was a Trojan prophetess, cursed by the god Apollo never to be believed," said Jane, assuming the lady took as much interest in learning as she did.

"And your parents chose that name for you?" The landlady fixed Cassandra with a commiserating look.

"It's my mother's name too," said Cassandra, glaring at Jane.

"Ah. Oh well. Then I suppose it can't be helped." The lady was now laying the blame back on earlier generations, where it was due. Jane sniggered and even Cassandra smiled at the unintended rudeness. It appeared that their hostess had missed out on lessons in tact when growing up.

Mrs Hill turned into a narrow landing and opened the door to what looked like a closet. A steep staircase rose ahead of her. "This is the way to the top room. Would you mind going up by yourself? It is rather a squeeze for me. I usually send the maid."

Jane went first as the slimmest, but her height meant she had to crouch down. Cassandra scrambled up behind, going sideways so as not to catch her hips.

"It's like a secret passageway to hide the papist priests from Queen Elizabeth's hunters," Jane said excitedly, swept up in the enchantment of a room that few could enter.

"But will there be a bed?" grumbled Cassandra.

Jane opened the door at the top of the stairs and found a cabin of a bedchamber with steeply sloping ceilings. She could stand upright in the middle but had to bend over if she wished to visit the corners. Two little beds were tucked under the eaves, a washstand in the middle. Best of all though was the window that looked out over the rooftops of Oxford. She could see the tower of a church and the spire of another, as well as the walls of the colleges. Trees nodded in all directions, promising gardens and parklands hidden behind the fortifications. From here you couldn't even see the bustle of the road beneath with the farmers and shopkeepers going about their business, though you could hear them. The girls were set apart in their own little tower.

Jane turned on the spot, arms outstretched. "See: plenty of room. I imagine Frank will envy us this space once he gets his commission." Their brother, who lay between them in age, was bound for the navy now he had finished at naval college. "He only gets a hammock's length."

"I bag the bed on the left." Cassandra felt the sheets to check they weren't damp. Their mother had also warned them of the perils of catching a chill from inadequately aired linen. In her presence the girls might sigh and roll their eyes over her pronouncements, but once away from home they had to admit she was often right.

Jane didn't mind which bed she took. The one left to her was under the window. Of course that likely made it colder, but it was only September and she didn't yet have to worry about being frozen overnight by a draught.

"Is everything to your satisfaction?" called their hostess.

"Yes, thank you, Mrs Hill," replied Cassandra.

"Very well. Dinner will be served downstairs in half an hour. You'll hear the clocks strike five." Her footsteps marked her retreat back downstairs.

Jane flopped on the bed. It was an unyielding surface – a horsehair mattress in all likelihood. Maybe there would be time for a nap?

Cassandra poked her.

"We have to dress for dinner."

"O Prophetess, I don't believe a word you say," teased Jane.

Cassandra rested her fists on her hips. "And I haven't heard that joke before."

"The old ones are the best." Jane laced her fingers together across her stomach.

"You know we have to change. We've been travelling all day. We must look like frights!"

"Really? Mother's not here to see if we've put on a clean fichu." Jane patted her clothing, noting that her muslin scarf was somewhat rumpled after a day's travel. The Austen sisters wore them across their chests and tucked into their belts to make the scooped necks of their gowns suitable for travelling daywear.

"Our trunk is here so you've no excuse." Cassandra undid the buckles.

"Haven't I?"

"Think of the poor man who had to squeeze up here with this. He must've had to put it on his back like a snail."

When described like that, Jane decided she should honour the servant's effort by changing for dinner as the company expected.

"In any case, you never know who we'll meet at dinner," continued Cassandra, opening the lid.

Jane bit her tongue, knowing where her sister's thoughts were going. A new place with interesting people was always Cassandra's hope, a wider society than that offered by the country. And if one among them proved to be a dashing fellow who would naturally be in want of a pretty, well-mannered wife, then all the more reason to wash off the day's travel and present the best appearance that they could muster.

Corrections to their clothing dutifully made, the two sisters ventured downstairs as the clocks of the city struck five. The rumble of voices led them to the narrow dining room on the first floor.

"Shall we go in?" asked Cassandra.

Jane gulped and nodded.

Chapter 6

Cassandra preceded Jane into the room and stopped as the gentlemen at the table rose. There were two – an elderly man and a younger, though fortunately neither possessed the kind of looks that would turn Cassandra into a silly goose. An older lady, possibly the wife of the senior man, remained seated but smiled a welcome. Their landlady came in with a covered dish.

"Ah, here are the girls. Country bred, so don't mind their manners too much. They are to be with us for a few days," said Mrs Hill, continuing with her habit of saying things that could be construed as insults if she had not thrown them out with no sign she meant to offend. "Mr and Mrs Lambton, Mr Herbert, this is Miss Austen and Miss Jane Austen."

The girls dipped a curtsey then moved to the remaining seats.

"Mr Herbert is the Secretary to the Oxford Canal. He is staying here while they complete the works," Mrs Hill explained. "The Lambtons are from Wantage in Berkshire. They are visiting their son who is also at St John's." Mrs Hill beamed at them with pride. "Mr Lambton is a magistrate, you know; he locks people up left, right, and centre."

Mr Lambton, who was as mild as his name suggested, looked alarmed by this statement. "Oh I say, Mrs Hill."

"I believe our Michael rows with your brother Henry, Miss Austen," said Mrs Lambton to Cassandra, keen to change the subject away from her husband's decisions in the local courts of their district. And thus, the lady and Cassandra went off on an easy conversation about the river and sporting achievements (it would appear Michael had many and cast all other nineteen-year-olds into the shade).

Jane had been left with the place next to the Secretary. He did not look thrilled to be seated by the girl barely out of childhood rather than the pretty young woman Cassandra, but he gave Jane a polite smile nonetheless.

"It must be a big change for you to come to a city into society like this," Mr Herbert said. "The number of young men in residence is no small attraction to a young lady, though you've a few years yet before you need worry about that, of course. Have you been to Oxford before?" He offered her the dish of potatoes.

Jane scooped up a little, not sure she liked his tone and assumption that she thought of nothing but young suitors – that was more Cassandra's kind of thing, and her sister had many more interests than attracting a beau, for all Jane's teasing on the subject. "Yes, sir. I was at school here briefly when I was little." That brought back those dark days. The memories were not happy ones, far worse than the experience she had had at her school in Reading.

"Then you must have fond reminiscences of the place." He gave her a bland smile and looked down at his plate, evidently feeling as though he had done his part in making some remark.

"Oh yes," Jane said sourly. "We were chased away by an infectious fever and almost died. Our friend's mother, who came to rescue us, caught it and did die. Happy days indeed." Perhaps she shouldn't have used that sardonic tone, but it annoyed her when everyone assumed a child experienced school as unclouded sunshine.

His attention pricked, he turned back to her. "Forgive my assumption. My own schooldays, long ago though they might seem to you, are among my fondest memories."

Jane relented. The poor man had been attempting to be friendly, finding a topic he could share with a girl so much younger than he was. "It is natural to think so, sir. Tell me, Mr Herbert, what does being a secretary to the canal involve?"

"*The* Secretary." He reached for another dish. "I ensure the smooth running of the works, arranging for men and materials to be available so we can complete it on time, doing all the business arrangements, arranging loans," he caught himself mid-flow and considered his audience, "but you needn't worry your little head about that. I expect you are attracted by the romance of the project linking the north to the southern parts of the kingdom?"

Jane was tempted to measure her head with her hands to find out just how little it was in truth. He seemed under the impression she couldn't keep anything very complicated inside it. "That does sound ambitious. When will it be finished?" Jane helped herself to a spoonful of peas.

"We aim to open at the start of the next year: begin the 1790s as we mean to go on. Progress, commerce, a wealthier nation!"

She nodded. "That sounds very…" she searched for the right word, "fulfilling. To know that you are creating something new and leaving behind a legacy."

He sat back in his chair. "Indeed, but, my, my, you give your opinion very decidedly for so young a person."

Jane grimaced. "I'm afraid it is the way we are all brought up to speak in our household. Papa enjoys a good debate."

"How novel."

Jane wasn't sure if Mr Herbert approved. "I hope I did not offend you?"

His lips stretched in a smile. "Not at all, Miss Jane. A slice of mutton?"

Oh dear: she had offended him. Jane took the mutton and fell silent.

However, a little later, Mr Herbert showed that he didn't hold a grudge that she was impertinent for her age. When he learned from Cassandra that they had decided on an excursion to view the works the very next day, he insisted that he act as their guide.

"No really, it is in my remit," he said, holding up a hand to cut off Cassandra's protests that he must be too busy. "I am often asked to show prospective investors around."

"I think you might be disappointed in how much either of us has to invest," murmured Jane, thinking of her purse, which was home to more hairpins than it was coins.

"But well-bred young ladies have such interesting connections!" He raised his glass to them both. "I insist."

Cassandra bowed her head in agreement, then shrugged so that only Jane noticed. Indeed, once an adult insisted on making themselves helpful, there was nothing the girls could do. Besides, an informed guide would appeal to her father and Henry. Neither had much money to invest as far as Jane knew, but perhaps they might be persuaded to part with a little? Even in Steventon she had heard talk that canals were the English gentleman's favourite speculation.

After dinner, they took a note over the road to the lodge so it could be delivered to their father, informing him of the slight alteration to their plans. They could see that the candles were lit in hall where Henry and Papa were dining, the voices coming from the open doors loud and happy, the laughter rumbling like thunder. A snatch of song rose up and fell away.

"I wish we could join them," said Jane wistfully, twisting a lock of hair around her index finger. "Don't you wish you could be a student?"

Cassandra nudged her. "Tired of me already, are you?"

"No!" Jane protested. "Never!"

Cassandra took her arm and tugged her away. "Let's go back and you can read one of your stories to me. Who needs dinner in a college when they have a story by Jane Austen to digest?"

Spirits lifted by that suggestion, the Austen girls returned to their chamber at the top of the house.

For Frank Austen (enclosed in a letter to Mrs Austen)

My dear Frank,

I thought you would enjoy an illustration of the contents of my little head (according to the

Secretary of the Oxford Canal) as drawn in profile by Cassandra. Please note the prominent place given to my intelligence and education, as well as his acknowledgment that marriage is always at the back of any girl's mind as we navigate our vital business of ribbons, dresses, and dancing.

Before you write back with your agreement to this description being highly accurate, I would just mention that Cassandra is currently drawing up an illustration of the contents of your own head. So far we have filled it with "Teasing your sisters", "Sea matters", and not much else.

Yours affectionately,

Jane

Fluff Ribbons
Kittens
Duty Dresses
Religion
Letter Writing
Dinner Opinions Dogs
Void Jokes Education
Balls
Novels
Family Hot Chocolate Confectionery
Politics
Dancing
Scandals

Chapter 7

Mr Austen, Henry, and Jenkinson arrived at the lodgings shortly after the girls had finished their breakfast. Grandison trotted at their heels and Jane detected a particularly pleased air about her hound, his tongue poking out in a happy pant.

She got down on her knees to greet her canine friend. "Have you behaved well for Henry? Please say no." It would be the height of unfairness if Grandison suddenly started minding his manners as soon as he was out of her company.

"You will be overjoyed to hear, Jane, that he has disgraced himself as only a Dog-Austen could," said Henry gravely.

"Oh? How so?" She mock-frowned at the black-and-white spotted face of Grandison. His black eye patch gave him a piratical smile.

"Sausages," said her father with admirable control.

"Sausages?" wondered Jane.

"He stole…" began her father.

Henry raised a hand. "Perhaps he only borrowed? Can we not be charitable?"

"If borrowing consists of storing them in his stomach, then yes," muttered Jenkinson.

"Then let us call it a permanent loan," Henry announced.

Mr Austen chuckled. "Grandison took out on *permanent loan* the breakfast sausages meant for High Table. He was duly reminded that he is not of sufficient academic attainment to be worthy of a whole string, and his failing was made up for in the shape of a fine paid by his owner."

Jane gulped, considering the scanty contents of her purse.

"A fine paid by his *temporary* custodian," Henry corrected. "Do not fear, Jane, I took responsibility. My friends thought it all a great jest."

Jenkinson nodded enthusiastically. "We passed round a hat to contribute to Grandison's breakfast fund."

"They only considered it a joke because it wasn't their sausages that were taken," concluded Mr Austen. "We at High Table had to make do with ham. I fear he will not be welcome back as an overnight guest."

Further thoughts about breakfast meats were interrupted by the arrival of Mr Herbert, come for an introduction as had been arranged the evening before. The gentlemen bowed and exchanged suitable words of mutual delight at the opportunity. Jane wished they would hurry up and get on with the visit, as she was eager to see the canal about which she had heard so much.

"Mr Herbert, are you a university man?" asked Mr Austen as they made their way towards the canal offices down New Inn Hall Lane. Jane followed behind with Grandison on a leash.

"I didn't have that honour," said the Secretary. "No, sir, I had to work my way up the hard way."

"Very commendable," said Mr Austen.

Mr Herbert gave a little bow at the praise. "I was fortunate that my merits attracted the attention of my patron, a lawyer, well known in Oxford as having the best practice in the county. Mr Burgh took me on as his clerk. I eventually became his equal in the business, and it was my legal acumen that earned me the approbation of the shareholders in the canal."

"I imagine there are many complex legal issues to decide," said Mr Austen, humouring the man. Mr Herbert was what Jane's mother would call the bugler for his own regiment of one.

"Oh indeed, you probably could not imagine even half of them! The pasturage we have to persuade them to part with, the landowners who don't want the canal to navigate past their windows – and those that do for the ease of transporting their crops out and bringing in the coal. There are many interests to satisfy."

"And doubtless a man of such acumen as yourself is very fitted to the task?"

Jane and Cassandra exchanged a look. When their father adopted that tone, all the family knew he was really of a different opinion.

"Indubitably, sir. I point out the neatness of the arrangements, an improvement worthy of Capability Brown the great landscape gardener, as well as the great convenience of having a canal so close to their properties. Very many of them thank me for presenting the project in such a way as to make it appealing, opening their eyes, so to speak."

"Splendid." Mr Austen rapped the paving stones with his cane, a cheerful little tap-tap to end the conversation.

They reached the grand offices of the Canal Company, marked by a carved mermaid over the door. She was a rustic rather than a classical fish-lady, with a stocky body and fat tail, quite fitting to an English office in a provincial city. Entering, Jane was struck by the smell of beeswax and parchment. It could have been a lawyer's office or an architect's studio, as only the pictures of bridges and boats connected it to the world of cargo and coal that was its reason for existing. At the end of the corridor in the biggest room in the building, she glimpsed clerks sitting on stools, like monks of old eager to finish their illuminations. These men were bent over ledgers, quills scratching out the latest deliveries and orders, rather than saints' lives and Bibles. Light poured in from high windows. Mr Herbert led Jane's party into a room at the front of the building dominated by a polished table. This chamber smelled of tobacco, and she could picture the meetings held here by the board of directors in a fog of pipe smoke as they refashioned the country to their liking.

A housekeeper came in with refreshments for the guests: sherry for the gentlemen and raspberry cordial for the girls, set out on a tray lined with a fine white cloth. Jane noticed it because she worried that she might stain it with her drink. She made sure not to let any of it dribble down the side. As in a nursery rhyme Jane liked to sing, the housekeeper had music wherever she went, thanks to the jingling bunch of keys on her belt.

"Thank you, Mrs Younge," said Mr Herbert. The lady retreated with a nod to the company. "Now, let me show you our map. This will help you understand the truly visionary endeavour." He pulled a tube from a shelf and took out a rolled chart. With Henry's help, he unfurled it on the table and placed paperweights on each corner. Jane, standing at the front with Cassandra, was quick to recognize a map of England. Mr Herbert seized a little pointing stick and proceeded to act as their teacher. "See, young ladies, how the Oxford Canal is key to the success of the whole network," he enthused. "Looking north, it links to the Coventry Canal, then to the Trent and Mersey, which can take you all the way to Liverpool. Have you heard of that city? It is a place quite north of here."

Jane murmured that yes indeed she had heard of it vaguely. Cassandra swallowed a giggle. Henry shot them an amused glance.

"To the west, the Thames and Severn Canal reaches Bristol. Looking south-east, we connect to the River Thames and the capital. The canal makes Oxford into the hub of the country. No more perilous voyages on the North and Irish Seas to carry coal, pottery, and other goods. They can be loaded onto a boat at a quay outside the mine or factory, then drawn by a single horse along peaceful waterways practically to the doorsteps of the customer, most of it passing along our canal."

Henry nodded admiringly but Jenkinson looked sceptical. He plucked up the courage to ask a question, face flushed.

"Well, er, Mr Herbert, my… my father is an investor in the scheme. I believe he has even bought shares in my name."

"Really? Your surname, sir?"

"Jenkinson, from Derby."

"Ah, the esteemed Mr Jenkinson! It is an honour, sir. How is your father?"

"In good health, thank you. He did say over the summer that he had heard that another company are talking of attempting, or at least proposing, a d… different route from London through Northampton. Is that so, do you know?"

Mr Herbert winced but then gave Jenkinson a pitying look. "That's all it is: talk, sir! They have barely started discussions and, once we are completely open, I think you can trust that their investors will see that it isn't worth their coin to dig a channel scores of miles long while we provide such excellent service. Come, let me show you and then there will be no more talk of alternatives."

Chapter 8

Jane trailed behind with Cassandra and Grandison as the men duly followed their guide back out onto the street.

"Did you not think that Mr Herbert protested a little too much when Mr Jenkinson asked about another canal scheme?" asked Jane.

Cassandra shrugged. "I imagine every canal builder lives in fear that a more attractive one will come along, like the belle of the season being upstaged by a new rival."

Jane applauded her sister's comparison. "Exactly!"

They paused as a cart carrying bricks rumbled past, a shire horse straining in the harness.

"It's much easier for a human belle to beautify oneself in silk and jewels thanks to a dressmaker and hairdresser. Think of all the work and years involved in building something that is hundreds of miles long!" Jane's mind was still grappling with that snaking line on the map. At first glance, she would've said it was a river like the Thames or the Avon, but then she had to make the adjustment that it was entirely new, dug out by men with little more than shovels to aid them. "The pyramids of Egypt are nothing to this."

Cassandra smiled at Jane's awe. "But you've never seen the pyramids, Jane. I expect you'd be more impressed if you had once stood in their shadow with the desert behind them – one of the Seven Wonders of the World. Plus, they have lasted thousands of years. Who is to say how long the canals will last?"

Their debate was silenced by turning a corner to come upon the works themselves. The girls stood at the top of a slope overlooking a big pit. To their left rose the pudding-basin-shaped mound that was the old site of Oxford Castle and beyond that the prison; to the right, some way off, was the classical frontage of Worcester College; at their feet an ugly scar in the earth in which worked the navigators, or navvies, as the canal builders were known. The colleges of Oxford lay behind them, meadows and farms in front, stretching to some hills a mile or so away. As the porter had said, they were constructing a lake right in the heart of the city.

"This is the last piece in the canal, our *pièce de résistance!*" said Mr Herbert. "The wharf where the canal boats will end their journey. *Le fin du voyage.* The end."

Jane rolled her eyes at Cassandra but didn't need to say anything. The Austens agreed that resorting to French was a sure sign of pretension.

"And see down there?" He pointed at a group of grey-clad men who were roped together. "The Governor of the gaol has lent us his convicts. We believe it a happy combination of efficient use of resources and a demonstration to the men that there are better ways to expend their labour than on crime.

They are taught a lesson, and we get our canal built in record time!"

From the glint in his eye, this clearly interested Mr Austen. "Indeed, that does sound most enlightened of the Governor. A Mr Harris, isn't it?"

"Mr Daniel Harris: quite the most helpful of governors the prison has ever known," agreed Mr Herbert.

Mr Austen tucked his thumbs in his waistcoat pockets, his pigeon-chested stance that usually accompanied a pronouncement. "Too many prisoners are left with only soulless work to do. Here they can look out of their prison windows each evening and see the positive difference they are helping to make. I hope they take pride in it?"

"One would hope," said Mr Herbert, sucking his teeth. "Sadly, the most hardened among them are set in their ways, resentful of the chance they've been given."

"Fascinating. Let's go closer and ask them," suggested Henry, already moving towards the men.

"Henry!" called Mr Austen. "This is hardly appropriate with your sisters in our party!"

"Don't worry, Papa, I'll protect the convicts from them." Henry bounded off. Grandison pulled on the leash to follow, so Jane obeyed his urging. She too was eager to see the prisoners. The only really wicked men she had come across so far in her short life were ones in novels, and a writer should always be on the lookout for authentic experiences. Unless the prisoners were noblemen wrongly incarcerated, convicts in books tended to be rough types ready to do the dirty work of the villain. How thrilling to come across such people in Oxford, of all places!

Jane's slippers slid on the earth bank and only Cassandra's

quick move to support her elbow stopped her planting her bottom in the mud.

"Slow down," warned Cassandra. "I don't think you want your introduction to the convicts to be as muddy as they are."

"Girls, keep back!" said Mr Austen, clearly peeved that his son was forcing this encounter upon them. "What will your mother say?" he added under his breath, hurrying after Henry.

Jenkinson fell into step with the Austen sisters. "Never fear, ladies, I will protect you."

"We have Grandison for that," said Jane.

"But thank you," said Cassandra, always quick to spare another's feelings.

"Don't come any further!" said Mr Austen, walking across a deeper ditch on a plank.

The girls and Jenkinson stood on one side with Grandison as their guard, while the others in their party approached the warden whose job it was to keep an eye on the prison labourers. This man sat on a camp stool with his arms folded while the convicts dug at the bank. Seeing the gentry approach, he stood up and removed his cap. The prisoners paused in their labour, appearing happy to have an excuse to down tools.

"Do they look hardened types to you?" Jane whispered to Cassandra. The three convicts in this little work gang looked dirty, but they could hardly be blamed for that as they were digging up the soil. Their boots and stockings were caked with the stuff. Two men at the front came forward to talk to the visitors, sharp looks darting to Mr Herbert to see if he approved of what they were saying. He nodded like a headmaster with prize pupils. Jane noted that the convicts' smiles were overly broad and didn't reach their eyes. She sympathized: it had to be difficult to be happy when serving out a sentence of hard labour. One of them was missing his front teeth and had a flushed complexion – Jane imagined he might be a drunkard who had got into one too many fights and ended up on the wrong side of the law. He had a loud laugh and kept repeating "your honour" after every comment, like he was still addressing the judge that had sent him here. The other would've been a handsome fellow if he hadn't a sly look, befitting a renowned highwayman or cheat who cozened the gullible out of their worldly goods. His gaze slid to Jane and he winked. Jane looked away. She was right not to like that one.

The third man stood back, powerful hands resting on the handle of his spade, wide shoulders bowed. He had a shock of black hair, dirt-encrusted skin, and a furious frown which was directed at the visitors like they had personally insulted him. Jane's first impression was that he was the most dangerous of the three, as if he were barely suppressing his rage, and it occurred to her that her father was within reach of a blow from that spade.

"Papa, had we not better move on?" she called out. "Grandison is fretting."

The dog looked up at her, surprised to hear this. His tail swished arcs in the mud.

"You three take him to the canal path and we'll catch up with you," said her father, pointing out the track that led to the already finished part of the project. He seemed pleased to have an excuse to send his daughters away from such low society.

Jane didn't want to leave him behind, not with that spade so close. "We'd appreciate your company."

"I'll be along presently. Mr Jenkinson will look after you." Her father was not to be moved once his interest was engaged. He probably thought talking to the convicts a chance for some pastoral remarks to the sinners in God's flock, the lost sheep most worthy of his care.

"Come along, Jane," said Cassandra. The handsome convict was now leering at her. "We've seen enough."

The girls took a path of planks laid on the mud to climb out of the pit, Mr Jenkinson ready with a steadying arm in case either of them slipped. Workers wheeling barrows made way for them and murmured polite greetings. It seemed the labourers were used to sightseers and had instructions to be respectful.

"Would you like to work as a navvy if you were a prisoner?" Jane asked Mr Jenkinson as her thoughts lingered over the anger of the third man. "Or would you be resentful and bitter?"

"I hope, Miss Jane, that I would never be a convict and have to find out," said Mr Jenkinson.

"It is a 'what if'," Cassandra explained. "You have to get used to the way my sister's mind works. She comes up with these questions: what if you had a fortune of ten thousand a year; what if you were a captain of a ship, separated from the girl you loved by duty; what if you stole your parents' money and ran off with your beau…?"

Jane picked up the theme. "What if you were the owner of a haunted house? What if you found a casket containing a mysterious scroll? What if you were made homeless by your money-pinching relatives – would you go on stage or retire to a humble home in the country?"

Jenkinson looked puzzled by this blizzard of questions. "Goodness, Miss Jane, you really spend your time thinking up all these situations?"

Jane nodded. "Doesn't everyone?"

Cassandra chuckled. "You see, Mr Jenkinson, her question about the convicts is really quite normal for her." Both girls turned expectant eyes on him, waiting for his answer.

"I… I suppose I would prefer to do something useful with my time," he said at length. "If I were guilty of a crime, I would like to know that I could pay back my debt with labour outdoors where at least I can see the sky and feel the breeze, rather than sitting and contemplating my sins in a stuffy cell."

"Bravo, Mr Jenkinson," said Jane. "A very good 'what if' answer. You, Cassandra?"

Cassandra plucked a stalk of grass from the vegetation fringing the canal. The freshly beaten path was hedged on one side by bushes; on the other was the water along which a narrowboat was approaching, pulled along by a horse who was led by a lad. This section looked very new, the banks mainly mud with a few shoots of grass and weeds. "I think I'd scowl and huff like that third man, annoyed to be working hard for no pay. You, Jane?"

"I'd use it to plan my escape," said Jane quickly, having already thought it through. "That surely must be uppermost in most prisoners' minds?"

"Only the devious ones," said Jenkinson.

Both Austen sisters applauded this remark.

"A very good insult. Jane, Mr Jenkinson says you are devious," declared Cassandra.

"No, no, good gracious," spluttered Jenkinson. "I did not mean—"

"Don't spoil it now," said Jane, "when you are doing so well. Stand by your hit and I will allow you the point."

Jenkinson muttered something that sounded like "addling Austens", and the girls exchanged triumphant looks.

Grandison, meanwhile, had become very interested in the approaching horse. Jane had let him off the leash when they began the walk along the towpath so he could sniff at the scents to his heart's content without wrenching her arm off, but the boat proved more interesting. He gambolled towards the patient horse, barking merrily. The horse looked up in weary disdain and carried on plodding forward, such interruptions common in its life. Not so the little dog that lived on the boat. It shot out like a rocket, leaped to the bank, and berated Grandison in a sharp barrage of yips for daring to woof at the horse.

"Oh dear." Jane hurried forward, leash at the ready to restrain her excited hound. "Grandison, behave!"

The little dog – a Jack Russell – nipped at Grandison's rear legs, which caused the normally peaceable hound to spin round and let out his most fearsome growl. The exchange of barks intensified and became a scrap, bloodcurdling snaps and snarls emitted by the two enemies. Jane felt the shame only a dog owner knows when their usually reliable hound turns into the worst version of themselves.

"Grandison, enough!" Her tone was shrill, but Grandison was locked in battle and unable to pay her any attention. Jenkinson was no help and Cassandra was keeping well back to preserve her muslin. Everyone was at a loss what to do.

Not so the lad leading the horse. He grabbed Grandison's collar with one hand and the scruff of the little dog's neck with the other and hauled them apart. He threw the Jack

Russell back on the barge with a command to "stay!" and dragged the still barking Grandison towards Jane.

"Control your dog, Miss!" he said, bright blue eyes meeting hers with an icy glare.

That was when Jane realized that the person she had thought was a lad was actually a lass in breeches.

Chapter 9

"I'm so sorry!" said Jane. "Grandison is not normally like that."

"Grandison?" The girl snorted in disdain as if to say that name summed up everything that was wrong with the gentry and their dogs.

Jane, from knowing she was in the wrong, now moved to feeling defensive of her pet. "Besides, it wasn't entirely his fault. Your dog started it."

"Rag-N'-Bone did not start it! He was defending his territory!" The girl's scruffy blonde hair was cropped short and her shirt patched, but she stood like a general sure of her ground. She had her guns trained on Jane and Grandison and was not retreating.

Jane did not want to lose momentum for her argument by pausing to acknowledge the inventive name for the Jack Russell. "And Grandison was attempting to make friends!"

"By charging Nettlebed?" The girl's lip curled.

Another interesting name. "He was approaching with enthusiasm, but I would say that 'charging' is an exaggeration."

"You *would* say that, wouldn't you?" The lass was now scowling at Jane's companions. "And I don't doubt that your friends will make it our fault too. The canal folk are always blamed for everything around here." She waved to the cottages that stretched to the water, the end of their gardens cut off by the canal. "Can't move an inch without someone calling for the local magistrate."

"I wasn't blaming you!"

"You blamed my dog, and that means me."

"Well then, same here! You blamed Grandison." Jane crossed her arms and scowled. The girl crossed her arms and scowled back.

Cassandra lightly touched Jane's elbow. "Jane, dear, she did end the fight rather skilfully: you should thank her." She nudged her. "Go on."

Drat her sister! Conscience was an unwelcome arrival at that interesting moment in an argument.

"Thank you," Jane gritted out through clenched teeth.

Her magnanimity was not rewarded, which made it even more humiliating.

"Hah! Some of us have work to do." The girl picked up the horse's halter that she had dropped and proceeded to ignore them. Grandison wagged his tail and butted her with his nose, having quite forgotten that he was a hellhound, but the girl just pushed him away. "Get on with you."

Jane took that as an instruction to them all and started to walk off, conscious she hadn't come out well from that encounter. At that moment, a man came out of the cabin of the narrowboat, took stock of the situation, and removed his cap. He had the same blue eyes and dark blonde hair as his daughter, though there the resemblance stopped, as he had a shaggy beard and moustache and moved with the lumbering gestures of a bear.

"Sir, Misses, I hope my daughter isn't bothering you?" he said, his voice with the intonation of the town of Birmingham, an accent that turned "i" into "oy".

Jane took satisfaction in seeing the girl's face take on an even more furious cast.

"Georgie means no disrespect." He fumbled the brim of his cap. "Believe me, sir, we wants no trouble here." His eyes were now on Mr Herbert, Henry, and Mr Austen who were hurrying to catch up with them.

Arguing with a girl her own age was one thing, possibly forgivable as it came with few repercussions. Seeing the man's obvious consternation that serious consequences might fall on them if their "betters" decided to complain to the canal owners, Jane repented of revelling in her rival's discomfort. She found a better Jane inside and brought her out.

"Please, sir, do not distress yourself. My dog and yours had a disagreement – a common enough happening, I dare say. No harm was done, no blood shed, just a lot of sound and fury, signifying nothing."

"Well then." The man stepped onto the bank and jerked his head at his daughter. "Go below, Georgina." He took the halter of the poor horse – the creature present to have conducted itself to the greatest credit. "I'd better be getting along, if that's all right with you. We have a delivery."

Jane nodded and started walking again. Cassandra caught her arm, disapproval plain.

"Be thankful Father wasn't there to witness that. He would be furious with you!"

Jenkinson was diplomatically gazing up at a flight of geese passing overhead.

Jane didn't need a scolding from Cassandra on top of her own guilty feelings. "I know. I shouldn't have lost my temper. But it was Grandison…!"

"You think he cares if a barge girl thinks poorly of him?"

Jane had to admit she had been absurd. "Do you ever tire of always being right?"

"Aha!" Her sister swung around to their escort. "You said it. Mr Jenkinson, you are a witness!"

He smiled. "I'm sorry, Miss Austen, my thoughts were quite elsewhere."

Cassandra narrowed her eyes. "Do you have sisters, sir?"

"Two, so I know better than to get between them. That's a tussle worse than Grandison and Rag-N'-Bone."

Jane clasped Cassandra's hand in hers and pulled her along, wanting to put the humiliating memory behind her. "What a splendid name! I almost forgave the girl her poor judgment when she revealed that. And Nettlebed!"

"She must work very hard for her living, poor thing," said Cassandra, casting a glance back to the narrowboat which was passing under a bridge.

"Poor thing?" Judging it safe, Jane let Grandison off the leash once more. He bounded off to greet Henry as he approached along the towpath. "I can't imagine anything more exciting than being a water gypsy, travelling the length of the kingdom. Even to Liverpool!"

"A place quite north of here," Cassandra finished solemnly. "Or so I've been told."

Chapter 10

That afternoon the girls and Mr Austen walked to another stretch of water of far older lineage: the River Thames. They took the road through the middle of Oxford to near Friar Bacon's Bridge. What drew them was a promise to watch Henry practise for his race. The St John's boat had eight oarsmen, and Jane was relieved to see that her brother was not responsible for steering. The honour of coxswain was held by another student, one with the stature of a jockey, who was to sit in the stern controlling the rudder. He scowled at everyone, including the girls and Grandison. His expression reminded Jane of their neighbour's kitchen cat, a creature she took care to avoid when visiting as he liked to scratch at ankles.

Waiting for Henry's crew to carry their vessel from the boathouse to the bank, Jane took a moment to appreciate the area chosen for the exercise. The river rippled between grassy banks, overhung by willows. Ducks arrowed across the water, hoping for crusts; moorhens waded in the shallower parts, green stockings flashing. A swan drifted past, regal head bent to admire its reflection. It looked a picturesque location for what was about to be a water battle of great ferocity. She kept a tight hold on her dog's leash so he didn't take it into his head to disturb the peace again by chasing so many delightful avian targets.

The students emerged, carrying the boat upside down. They looked like a massive water beetle with sixteen legs scurrying to the bank.

"On the count of three!" called Henry. On his signal, the boat was turned right way up, launched to sit impressively in the water, a little warship rocking on the waves.

The boat, Henry informed them, was the kind called a "coque", used by the navy in their own regattas on Plymouth Sound. Four rows of benches were fitted to accommodate pairs of oarsmen. His crewmates had already stripped down to shirt and breeches. Henry passed Cassandra his jacket and took off his cravat.

"Can't row trussed up like a chicken for the oven," he explained with a smile.

"I didn't realize the boats were so large," Jane said.

"Quite so, sister mine. They're a little big for the river to race side-by-side, so that is why the aim is to overtake the enemy," Henry said. His eyes glinted with that dangerous look of an Austen about to do mischief.

"The enemy?" asked Jane.

"The opposition," Henry corrected. "When we ram them—"

"Ram?" Cassandra looked alarmed.

"*Bump* into them," Henry went on smoothly, "we move up into their position in the league. The aim is to get to the top of the table and be declared the winner."

"Come on, Austen," snarled the coxswain. "Some of us have come here to train!"

Henry patted Jane's arm and jogged over to the boat. He jumped into his position and seized his oar.

"Starboard men, push off." On his order, the four oarsmen nearest the bank used their oars to propel the boat into the current. Once they were headed in the right direction, Henry lowered his oar.

"And stroke!"

The idea was for the men to all copy him, but two of them were not paying attention. Their oars clashed with their fellows' and the boat spun. Not the heroic beginning that Henry had probably hoped for in front of visitors.

"Lambton, Keir, pay attention!" barked the cox.

That had to be the Lambtons' sporting son, currently being cuffed by the man beside him!

"Have a good practice!" called Cassandra.

"You need it!" added Jane.

Mr Austen, meanwhile, had struck up a conversation with the college servant responsible for the boathouse. He returned to the girls with a spring in his step.

"See here, my dears, the boatman has some fishing tackle he can lend me. I'm minded to spend a few hours trying my luck just along the bank. He says the inlet where the River Cherwell joins the Thames is a good spot for perch. Will you amuse yourselves for the rest of the afternoon?"

"We will go to the shops and look for ribbons," said Cassandra quickly.

Jane groaned.

"Don't be like that: you know the selection here is going to be vastly superior to anything Steventon can offer us,"

Cassandra said in a low voice. "And you owe me after the embarrassment at the canal."

Jane sighed and nodded.

"You do that," said Mr Austen, not really paying attention now his thoughts had gone to the finny denizens, as he poetically termed the fish of the river. "Shops and dogs do not mix well, so I'll keep Grandison with me then call in at your lodgings later to check on you before dinner. Cassandra, look after your sister. Jane, behave!"

"Yes, Papa," they replied in unison.

"We didn't properly thank Mr Herbert for his kindness in showing us around this morning. I think it only fitting to invite him back to dinner at St John's." He was already walking off, Grandison beside him, anticipating a pleasurable afternoon sitting on the riverbank.

Jane sighed. "And so we are abandoned by our menfolk."

Cassandra laughed. "You can't pretend you are disappointed, Jane. Fishing holds no attractions for you."

That was true. "I would've happily taken an oar and gone for a boat trip. It is so unfair girls aren't allowed to form teams like Henry's. It looks fun."

Her sister took her arm. "Let's go look at ribbons."

"See? The unfairness continues." Jane pretended to drag her feet, but she didn't really mind looking at what the shops had to offer. She liked ribbons as much as the next girl. Everything was so different in a city, so much choice compared with the limited range of things she'd seen a hundred times in the peddler's pack or little shops near her home.

Cassandra proved she had not wasted her time at the dinner table last night because Mrs Lambton had already told her the best places to go for trimmings.

"She told me that there used to be two excellent shops in which you could buy material, but one of them closed recently so we won't have as much choice," she explained. She guided Jane with confident steps up to the High Street, turned down an easily missed alley, and into the dress shop. Cassandra's head for maps was much improved when she had the reward of a draper's to fix her attention. Bolts of muslin, woollen cloth, and cotton lay stacked like geological strata behind the counter. Ribbons dangled enticingly from revolving racks, fluttering in the breeze from the open door like kite strings. Two women pored over fashion plates spread out on the counter, debating the merits of puffed sleeves or straight as the shop assistant looked on benignly. They turned to him to give a final verdict.

"I recommend straight. Much more economical with the cloth," he said, having sized up with his expert eye the purses of his customers. They agreed and he began measuring out the yardage required, whisking the cloth through his fingers with the ease of experience. Jane coveted the cloth, thinking how many dresses she could make out of it, but fine stuff was expensive, and she could only hope for one or two lengths a year from her pin money.

Cassandra felt the quality of a length of blue satin ribbon. "This would look very well on your best bonnet."

Jane touched the ribbon lightly. The colour was like the summer sky fallen to earth; it slipped and slid like butter through her fingers. "It's beautiful, but I can't afford it. My pin money is all spent."

"What did you spend it on?" Cassandra shook her head. "No, don't tell me: paper and ink. You would be the best dressed girl in England if you could write your way into a gown."

"Oh, how splendid!" Jane adored that idea; it would be like seeing a spell take form. "I would be able to conjure up such finery that Edward's family at Godmersham would not feel the slightest embarrassment at having his poor relations to stay." Their third eldest brother had been adopted as heir by their distant cousins, the Knight family, and was destined for much greater things than the rest of the Austen brood. He was expected to make a name for himself in high society, so his jacket and breeches were always the finest money could buy, tailored by top London establishments on Bond Street.

Cassandra laughed wryly, both aware of some excruciating moments during visits when they had been made to feel very lacking for their country ways. She turned to a less expensive display of trimmings.

Jane was no longer interested in following her sister's ferreting though the bargain tray, her mind on the strange fate that had befallen her brothers. She had never given much thought before to what happened to the minor characters in the fairy tales, the sons and daughters who didn't go on the quest, weren't beautiful or bold, or failed to answer the riddle correctly. With Edward whisked away to enjoy such a different style of living, of grand houses like some hero of a ballad taken by the Fairy Queen to her land, Jane's sympathy was now with those that were left behind. She loved Ned, of course she did, but it was hard not to feel a twinge of jealousy. Her oldest brother James never said a thing, nor did Henry complain, but it must have been galling not to have been picked when the opportunity could equally have been bestowed on them. As girls, she and Cassandra had always been destined to live unremarkable lives, remembered by few once they were gone, but she felt for her brothers to be so overshadowed by Edward.

The bell rang and a fresh-faced woman in a plain cotton dress came in. Jane judged her a farmer's wife up to do her shopping in the city, purse swelled by whatever produce she had sold at market. She moved along so the newcomer could consult the assistant on the best material for workaday aprons. Jane's fingers wandered to a tray of buttons that looked like a dragon's hoard of jewels. One plain brown one, slightly chipped, had fallen into the mix.

And then there was poor George, mused Jane, her second brother whom she'd only met once or twice. Her parents said he had been a simple-minded fellow from birth, and so destined to stay on the farm where he was sent as an infant. They said he was happier there than in the rectory, but Jane wondered how they knew. Life was never fair. Her fingers rested on a button in the shape of an anchor. Just as well Frank and the baby of the family, Charles, were mad to go into the navy. No older brother would follow them there to cast a shadow. They could forge their own path. Perhaps they could become famous through daring deeds? That would appeal to the novel-reading Austens who loved tales of bravery and adventure.

The farmer's wife's voice rose a notch. Alert for anything of interest, Jane could not help overhearing. "In prison! I've never been more shocked in all my life." The woman fanned herself with a fashion journal, cheeks flushed raspberry red.

"I'm surprised you had not heard," said the assistant, clearly relishing his role of serving up gossip to someone not in the know. His tone was a little superior. "He was committed at the last assizes. Ten years."

The farmer's wife sank on a stool put there for customers who planned to stay for a while. "Heavens above! I find it hard to believe that Mr Gardiner would do such a thing. Mr Gardiner! He was such a pleasant fellow."

"That's a lesson to us all," the assistant said sanctimoniously. "From respected shopkeeper to canal navvy, from what I've heard. You can see him, ankle-deep in mud, paying his debt to society. He attracts quite an audience."

"I always thought he had a shifty look to him," chipped in another customer, drifting over to join the scandalmongers. "Such a gruff man, big hands measuring out the muslin like a lady's maid. There was something not right about that. Didn't I say, Janet?"

Her poor companion looked surprised to be so consulted, but she rallied and quickly swore that her friend had been very perceptive and foretold the disaster.

"I have to say he was always civil to us, even though we were his main rivals," said the assistant, nodding across the passage to a building that had been shuttered. The name "Gardiners" had been painted out, but Jane could still see the black letters faintly beneath the whitewash. "Mr Lucas was quite cut up to hear that he had been duped into thinking Gardiner an honest man. They'd even done business with each other, going to the warehouses in London when the Indiamen sailed into dock with their cargos. They used to bargain together for a better price – that was before this all came out."

Jane wondered what the unfortunate man's crime had been. Thankfully, the farmer's wife was consumed by the same curiosity. "Pray tell, what did he do?"

"Cheated the Canal Company." The assistant snipped off the cloth with a swift movement of the shears. "They gave him the contract to supply the very best drapes and linens for their headquarters, but when the accounts were checked, it was discovered that he had sent only the cheapest stuff and pocketed the difference."

"What a horrible thing to do!" said the farmer's wife.

The assistant nodded. "He swore that he'd sent the very highest quality, but the evidence of what was hanging at the windows and in the closets could not be gainsaid." The assistant parcelled up the cloth. "We, of course, got the contract to make up for the loss and Gardiner went out of business, his reputation ruined, as soon as the verdict went against him. His family had to leave town and go back to his wife's parents in Coventry. A cleverer man would've chosen a less prominent target to cheat than the Canal Company."

Jane looked back suspiciously at the buttons she had been examining. Was the gilt not wearing a little thin on the anchors?

"Very true," said the farmer's wife, getting up to go. "In addition to the brown, five yards of the blue serge, please, and matching thread. I'll be back to collect it later."

"Very good, madam." The assistant bowed and took the material down from its humble corner. "I'll have it waiting and, unlike Gardiner, you can trust us to make sure you get what you pay for." With this little quip, they parted, both satisfied.

In the end, Cassandra purchased a length of lace to edge the neck of her best shift. Jane had to hand it to the assistant: he took their money with no condescension in his tone. She had expected him to sniff with disdain.

"You came in to buy ribbons and come away with lace: there is a lesson about life in there somewhere," said Jane, dawdling behind her sister. Her eye had been caught by a bookseller's, but Cassandra tugged her onward.

"You have no money, remember?"

"True." Books were expensive and, in any case, it appeared the kind of place that would look down on novels, thinking the academics of the university wanted only history, philosophy, and other worthy tomes. Jane liked history but found it often left out the things she wanted to know about, such as how people used to live, and it mentioned very few women.

"Do you think we might've met the disgraced shopkeeper today?" asked Cassandra.

"It's possible, but I imagine there are quite a few prisoners in Oxford gaol." She had decided that the angry man was the most likely candidate, as he had the big hands that the lady had mentioned.

"How humiliating it must be to have lived as a person of good character and then find oneself exposed to your neighbours, doing hard labour as punishment," said Cassandra.

"That certainly is a harsh penalty."

"Perhaps it will shock him back to more honest ways?"

"If he ever gets the chance to return to ordinary life. Surely no one will give him employment or do business with him now? I know I wouldn't like to take the risk." Jane knew that in a society like Oxford, the punishment for a crime would go on far longer than time served. He was likely ruined for good. "He would have to move to somewhere he isn't known, like London."

"Or America. I'd go there. Cut ties completely and start again." Cassandra checked the street sign to ensure they were headed in the right direction.

"But you can't leave yourself behind. He might just fall into bad ways there too."

"You don't think he can change?" asked Cassandra.

"I doubt it. When someone lets me down, my good opinion once lost is lost for ever." They took a left past a church with a fine churchyard full of monuments and leaning tombstones.

Cassandra frowned. "I can't believe that of you. And what about the Christian duty to forgive?"

"Oh, I would forgive but I wouldn't forget."

Cassandra clucked her tongue. "I'm surprised you take such a hard line. I always thought you were ready to give people a second chance?"

Jane rather liked this high tone she had discovered. It was enjoyable to be like her father, sermonizing. Spending time in his company was rubbing off on her. "When it is the fault of a moment, naturally I would not hold it against them; but when a truly bad character is revealed, like deep-rooted dishonesty, I doubt much can be done. I've no wish to be taken for a fool."

"You are far from that – and I don't believe you are serious." Cassandra paused as they reached their lodgings. "If you are, O wise one, remember that we are also to love our neighbours as ourselves."

Jane nodded, not wanting to press the argument. Cassandra had a soft heart; Jane was always a little more satirical about their friends and neighbours. She prided herself on being able to sum people up with a few close observations, and she was yet to be proved wrong in her judgments. A flirt remained a flirt, a liar a liar, an angry man never learned to curb his temper: her father's parish was full of such examples. She didn't need to live in wider society to know that human character was harder than granite to reshape once it had taken a certain form.

"What do you think is for dinner?" she asked, changing the subject away from one on which Cassandra and she would not agree.

"Something plain." Cassandra entered the house.

"Served with a side dish of tactlessness," murmured Jane, anticipating the next set of putdowns from their hostess.

Chapter 11

Jane was rather disappointed that their father took Mr Herbert to St John's to dine, as she had hoped to get the Secretary's side of the story about the cheating shopkeeper. Any student of human nature could not help but be interested in what tipped a formerly good man over into such criminal and foolish behaviour. Usually, you could detect hints of their true nature before they went bad, like a bruise on an apple. She wanted to prove to Cassandra that she was right about the difficulty of changing your behaviour.

Cassandra listened patiently to Jane's thoughts on the subject. She lay on her stomach on the bed flicking through her diary.

"Jane, you steal sugar plums from the pantry. Grandison steals sausages. Are you sure you are really so superior?"

That observation caught Jane by surprise. She hadn't realized in her speechmaking she might have drawn a line and put herself on the wrong side of it. What excuse did she have for her forays into the pantry?

73

"I don't see that as stealing so much as advancing the treat to myself. Mama would give it to me eventually. It is not like she's a stranger that I'm stealing from."

"Are you sure that's not worse? And isn't the sin that of disobeying her? What are the Ten Commandments again?" Cassandra waggled her eyebrows.

They were written up on the wall at church so Jane could hardly pretend ignorance. "I do honour my parents. There is nothing in there about annoying older sisters though." Jane threw a rolled stocking at Cassandra.

Her sister caught it, much to their joint surprise as she was the family butterfingers. Cassandra opened her palm. "I hope this is a clean one?"

"Of course. I love you really."

"Meaning those you don't love would get dirty stockings thrown at them?"

Jane chuckled. "No. I wouldn't waste any time on them at all, let alone my stockings." She slumped down on her mattress. "Maybe you are right." Her short-lived career as a sermonizer had run its course.

Cassandra let out a hoot. "Second time in a day! This has to be a record. I'm writing it in my diary."

"You make it hard for someone to admit they are in the wrong!" grumbled Jane.

Cassandra closed her book. "Sorry. But what am I right about?"

"That I'm harder on the faults of others than I am on my own. I know taking plums is wrong, and I still do it. It's just that they are so..." Jane twirled her hand in the air.

"I know," groaned Cassandra, "and Mama always saves the best things for the boys. It's not fair. I tell myself that she knows we take them and doesn't really mind."

"You do it too?" Jane was aghast. She had thought she was the only one to sneak into the pantry and had always admitted it to her sister with a sense of nagging shame. She hadn't known Cassandra shared her sense that they were not fairly treated.

"Of course. It's a time-honoured tradition, started by James. He taught Ned, and Ned Henry. I would never have tasted one if I hadn't joined in."

It was Frank who had taught Jane to do it. She was sensing a pattern. "Don't tell me you taught Frank?"

"Naturally." Cassandra smiled complacently.

"Why didn't I know this?" Jane shook her head at her own ignorance.

"You may be the cleverest among us, Jane, but that doesn't mean you know everything; you just feel like you should."

Jane spread out like a starfish on the bed. "I'm shocked. I live in a family of trained thieves. There was I, feeling I had nothing in common with the prisoners, until I realized that the only difference between them and us is that the Austens haven't yet been caught."

"I hardly think Mama would cart us off to gaol," snorted Cassandra.

"I wouldn't be so sure," Jane said glumly.

At dinner, over a steaming bowl of cauliflower soup, the girls told Mr and Mrs Lambton how they had seen their son on the river with Henry.

"Isn't he a fine boy?" asked Mrs Lambton.

The young man too busy looking at the swans to remember his task? The boy who had made the boat spin and ruined Henry's heroic departure? Jane smiled down at her soup.

There was only one acceptable reply, however, which Cassandra duly gave. "We also took your advice and went to Mr Lucas's," she added.

Mrs Lambton cut a slice of bread from the loaf. "I hope you found what you were looking for?"

"We were well satisfied, thank you."

Jane saw another chance to sate her curiosity about the criminal shopkeeper. She doubted the company would resist the chance to discuss the case. "We were just saying that it is such a shame that Gardiner's had to close. Our mother says it is always better to be able to compare prices."

"Gardiner's!" scoffed Mrs Hill. "All of us are still feeling very sore about that! I have never been so let down since Mrs Decker stole one of my lodgers!"

"Oh?" asked Mrs Lambton. "What happened to Gardiner's? I only heard that they were closed."

"Much worse than that," Mrs Hill said darkly. "He was a swindler – swapping out good stuff for cheaper and pocketing the difference."

"He did this to you?" asked Jane.

Mrs Hill looked taken aback. "Well no, not that I noticed. Besides, he knew I wouldn't fall for such tricks. He kept them for places where the purchasers would not know any better. He couldn't fool us Oxford women and didn't try."

"Hmm," said Jane.

"We might've seen him today – from a distance," added Cassandra, "when we visited the canal works. There were convicts digging out the big basin."

"One would think they were digging to that new island Captain Cook discovered – what is its name?" mused Mrs Hill.

"New Holland," said Jane. "Botany Bay."

"I've heard talk that the government might send convicts there, now that the Americas no longer take our felons," said Mr Lambton, showing that he was paying attention to the conversation despite the folded newspaper by his plate. "Perhaps your linen draper could start a new life among those whatyoumacall'em?"

"Settlers?" suggested Cassandra.

"Natives?" tried Mrs Lambton.

"Kangaroos?" ventured Jane.

He pointed a fork at her. "Yes, that's them exactly. The Whatsits. Saw Stubbs' picture of the beast in Cook's diaries. Extraordinary. Babies in pouches like a pocket watch in my waistcoat!"

Having reached the subject of exotic creatures, the convicts were forgotten by all apart from Jane, as they discussed the various wonderful animals they had seen in pictures or as part of the travelling shows that toured the country. Cassandra enthused about the elephant she and Jane had met during a previous adventure in Reading, but Jane was more interested in the specimens of human nature she had encountered today.

A man who cheated the Canal Company now forced to work for them – that sounded like poetic justice, and she could imagine her father's opinion on the subject. Yet from Mrs Hill's words it was likely a first offence – or the first detected. Was there more to the story?

Jane sighed and stirred her soup. Curiosity was a burden she bore. Such mysteries were like a loose milk tooth that she had to wiggle until it fell out. It seemed that their stay in Oxford now had another little challenge for her to extract.

To Frank – Enclosed in a letter to Mrs Austen

Dear Frank,

After the map of my head, I thought you might be illuminated by the furthering of our knowledge of the wider world thanks to the clever people we meet here in Oxford. Herewith is a map of New Holland, courtesy of our esteemed houseguest, Mr Lambton. I'm sure you will find it extremely helpful if your voyages for His Majesty's Navy take you to the Antipodes.

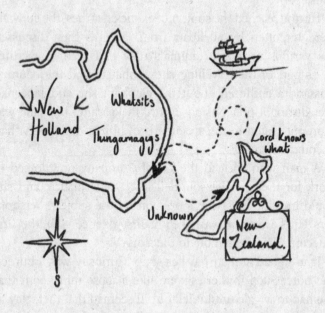

I'm sure such a detailed account of what you might find there will stand you in good stead with your future shipmates.

Yours affectionately,

Jane

Chapter 12

Having secured the return of her dog – though she loved Henry, a second night without Grandison was not to be borne, and there was the matter of the sausages – Jane resumed the usual duties of an owner. That meant the next morning saw her rising early to walk Grandison. Cassandra refused the invitation to accompany her by pulling the covers over her head.

All right then, thought Jane mutinously, *I'll go alone.*

There was no one up to stop her venturing out with only Grandison for company. If her mother had been there, she would have berated Jane for even considering walking about a strange city on her own.

But I'm not on my own, thought Jane, clipping the leash on Grandison. *As Mrs Hill points out, I'm a country girl, used to country ways of going about, not worried what others will think. And what danger could there possibly be at six in the morning?*

Her footsteps took her back to the canal. She had decided that it was the most fascinating new development she had ever seen and was worth a second look. Mist hung in the air, curling off the water. The world was changing, places becoming so much closer together than before. The heady speed of the mail coach with its team of horses might outstrip the narrowboat with its single horse, but the new possibility to move yourself lock, stock, and barrel on a canal from one end of the country to the other with very little bother was enchanting. She gazed down at the muddy water, considering how this was the same view for miles: strip of scrubby grass, water, towpath, and hedge, all the way north. The only interruptions were locks, a few tunnels, and aqueducts. Some of those latter were said by the newspapers to be quite spectacular, but the Oxford Canal, running through low-lying ground, had not required such feats of engineering. What a wonderful age she was living through!

Grandison was surprised to find his mistress standing still on the brick bridge that spanned the canal and not taking him somewhere to run off the lead. After tugging a few times to test her, he then resigned himself to let her look her fill.

"See those narrowboats, Grandison?" She petted his head. "Most of the cargo space is full of coal, but they have a little cabin for the boatman at the back. It must be like living in a gypsy caravan, but on water." The boat that was passing under the bridge was painted with roses and castles, as well as a landscape of lakes and mountains on the side of the cabin. "I wonder if that is a picture of the place it came from?" She had always imagined the lands of the north of England to be truly magnificent – snow-capped hills and dark chasms that resounded with the roar of waterfalls, like in the stories her family adored.

Wreathed in mist, everything seemed exceptionally romantic this morning. The boatman leading his horse was dressed in a thigh-length smock like a carter, though he had added a green ribbon to his squashy hat. He glanced up and touched his cap to her. She waved back.

"Going far?" she called.

"Back to Coventry, Miss."

"Is that a long way?"

"A fair step, but Robin will take us there safely." He rubbed the nose of his patient horse. "Good day to you."

"Goodbye!" Jane watched as the boatman and his Robin plodded north along the canal bank. She was interested to see what happened when two boats had to pass each other. The answer was that it involved lifting the rope of one boat over the roof of the other while exchanging news and gossip. Everyone was kept moving all the time to make their delivery deadlines, but the walking pace speed of the boats allowed each exchange to last a minute or two.

You must see the same faces again and again, thought Jane, a little community on the canal bank.

She watched the friendly boatman exchange a few words with the sour-faced man coming into Oxford. Her boatman didn't linger but urged Robin onwards.

"See that? How convenient," Jane told Grandison. You didn't have to sit in a parlour and endure an unwanted visit but could do a swift hail and farewell, with the excellent excuse that you had to get on. She imagined life as a boatman's daughter, sitting in her cabin with no bothersome visitors coming to tea, writing her stories inspired by the passing people and places. Perhaps Papa would like a change of career?

She chuckled at the idea. Her father would veto the suggestion, as there would be no room on the cramped vessel for a library. Her mother would have kittens at the thought of uprooting the Austen family for a life on the water. Families of their class were tied to their house and land – unless they joined the navy, of course.

"You again."

Jane turned in surprise to be so bluntly addressed. Grandison stood up, tail wagging. The girl from the barge had approached without Jane noticing, a can of milk in her hand. She must have been on an errand at the local dairy.

"Yes, me again," Jane said brightly.

"Can't keep you away, can we? You like watching other people work?"

"Actually, I do. It's fascinating."

Georgie seemed taken aback by Jane's frank admission. "Oh. Well then." She made to move on, her insult having failed to land as Jane was in such a good humour.

Jane skipped alongside. "I apologize for yesterday. I lost my temper." Jane no longer felt the urge to defend Grandison. If her foolish dog had decided the barge girl was a friend – and the tail wagging suggested he did – then who was she to hold grudges?

Georgie smirked. "So did I."

"I hope I didn't get you in trouble with your father?"

"No, he was worried Mr Herbert would take him to task for disrespect to our betters." Georgie's lips curled. "Local people don't trust us – think we bring trouble into their quiet city."

As the girl was being friendly today, Jane fell into step beside her. Georgie headed down the slope to the towpath.

"Quiet?" said Jane. "I think they aren't being very truthful if that's what they're claiming. Ask them about the Town and Gown Riots. And I dare say the students aren't the most peaceful members of local society, not if my brother is anything to go by."

"They have riots? In Oxford?" Georgie headed towards the end of the canal near the basin. As Jane could make her way back to her lodgings from there, she followed.

"Oh yes. A long time ago, but people died. I would think the boatmen very small beer compared to that."

"Doesn't stop them hating us and blaming us for every missing chicken or bit of trouble at Heyfield's Hutt." Georgie lifted the milk can out of sniffing reach of Grandison.

Jane moved to put Grandison further away from temptation. "What is Heyfield's Hutt?"

"A tavern. It's well known for its card games. Dad says the players are thieves and cardsharps. He wouldn't dream of going near it. It's up yonder." She pointed over her shoulder to the north. "We prefer to overnight down here. It's safer. Quieter."

Jane had to admit there were few people around, certainly no one who looked like a ne'er-do-well cardsharp, more's the pity.

"What do you think of this stretch?" asked Georgie with what seemed proprietorial interest. Jane supposed that boat people probably did feel they had a stake in what was effectively their home. "Brand spanking new it is. Wasn't open last time we were this way."

Jane could see that the banks were still little more than mud, the greenery not having yet taken hold. "Not very pretty, is it?"

"They've only just finished the puddling and filled it with water."

"What's puddling?"

"That means lining the channel – making it waterproof with a special mix of clay. That's what they're doing at the basin."

Jane remembered the exceptionally muddy nature of the task. "Oh, I see."

"It won't take long for it to settle. There will be grass for the horses to munch, and cow parsley, nut bushes – nature comes back quickly once the navvies move on."

Praising the canal and canal people seemed to be the secret to her companion's goodwill, so Jane obliged. "I can see that. The meadows either side are already very lovely."

"They're called the Bear Meadows – Great and Little." Georgie seemed pleased to know something the visitor didn't.

"Like the stars?"

Georgie laughed. "Maybe, but Dad said they were named after the tavern in Oxford."

Jane sniffed. That seemed a low thought; hers was more picturesque. "I prefer my suggestion."

"That's because you haven't walked beside a horse on a baking hot day dreaming of the next chance to wet your whistle. Many a boatman dreams of the next public house." They had reached Georgie's boat, announced by the eager barking of Rag-N'-Bone. "This is us." Now Jane had leisure to admire it, she could see that the boat was kept freshly painted in a livery of green, red, and yellow. Bells and flowers twined around the name.

"The *Mary-Ann*?" she asked.

"Dad named it after my mother." Georgie brushed the paintwork tenderly.

"And she's...?"

The boat girl turned away, back to business. "She died, ten days after giving birth to me. That's why I'm on the water. Dad had to take me with him." Georgie spoke brusquely, refusing to get sentimental.

Jane thought that he probably could have placed the baby with another family, paid for her to be looked after, like George on the farm, but held her tongue. "That must've been hard for him – and for you."

Georgie grinned. "Tied me to the cabin doorknob so I didn't fall in, but I learned quick enough not to do so. I was leading Nettlebed by the time I was four. Never fallen in – not once in all my years!"

Glimpsing a little stove and neatly made bunk through a porthole, Jane would have loved an invitation to come on board and see how the family arranged their living quarters, but Georgie didn't look as though her new friendliness would stretch that far.

"I'd better be going then," said Jane reluctantly. "They'll be wondering why I'm not at breakfast."

"Hah." The sound expressed how Georgie thought it nice for some that they had breakfast waiting for them when she had to fetch her own.

"Thank you for telling me about the canal," Jane said.

Georgie stepped onto the boat. "Fair warning: I'm about to let Rag-N'-Bone out of the cabin." The scrabbling claws indicated his exit would be as enthusiastic as the day before.

"Understood. See you later maybe?"

"Not if I see you first." But Georgie was smiling.

Jane took her dismissal in good part. She'd got more out of Georgie than expected. Perhaps next time she could ask what it was like to wear trousers?

Chapter 18

Jane's path back to her lodgings took her past the canal basin. Though it was still early, the convicts were already hard at work on what she guessed must be "puddling" – there were certainly lots of puddles! It looked like cold and miserable work, floundering around in the mixture of earth and clay that was meant to keep the water from seeping away. Others could wax lyrical about the golden fruits of the canal system, but for the poor men who had to do the hard work, Jane thought it must taste like the rotten berries of the Slough of Despond, the most miserable place in a favourite adventure tale, *The Pilgrim's Progress*. The angry-looking man, whom Jane suspected was the disgraced shopkeeper, hobbled to the water jug, the chain between the manacles on his ankles clinking. His head had been shaved recently, his scalp grey with bristles, scratched and cut from a blunt razor. Muscles bulged at his neck as he stooped to take a drink – definitely not someone to meet on a dark night! Grandison whined. Lifting his head slowly, the convict scowled at her as if her gaze were an insult. He then hissed at the dog.

If looks could kill, both she and her dog would be slain where they stood. Jane stepped back and Grandison barked sharply.

The guard looked up. "Gardiner, what you doing over there? Back to work!"

"Wretched, addle-pated Misses," Gardiner muttered.

"You won't want me to come and get you!" roared the warden.

"All right, all right, keep your hair on. I was just taking a drink." The man threw down the ladle. It sailed past the pail and landed in the mud. He turned his back contemptuously on the mess he had made.

"Oi! Pick that up!" The warden had his hand on his cudgel.

Turning with impudent slowness, Gardiner picked the ladle from the ground, wiped it on his already filthy shirt, and hung it on the side of the pail. "I'm not a sideshow for your amusement, girl!" he growled in an undertone to Jane.

"I never thought you were," Jane replied.

Convict and girl parted ways: Jane back to her breakfast and Gardiner to his punishment.

As she walked off, feeling his gaze like the heat of a furnace on her back, she wished she had come up with a better retort, but words were easier to shape on paper than in the moment. She tried to lift her spirits by defiance.

"He looks mean," she told Grandison. "Don't you agree?"

Grandison wagged his tail, which, to be honest, was his view on most things in life.

"He's just a mean old man. I have taken a firm prejudice against him," she went on. "He scowled at me as if I were yelling insults when all I did was look down at the works. I was interested in puddling. I can't be to blame if he chose that moment to take a drink. I refuse to be scared of him."

Grandison woofed.

Determined her attitude would not change, she headed in for breakfast.

"Jane, where have you been?" asked Cassandra when she noticed the state of Jane's shoes and Grandison's paws.

Jane kneeled in the back kitchen, using a rag to clean first the dog, then her own feet. There was a lot of repetition in the duties of a dog owner in a muddy autumn. "Along the canal." She debated whether she should tell Cassandra all that had happened or only a select part.

"Mother wouldn't like that!" Cassandra frowned, belatedly remembering she was the elder and therefore the more responsible.

Jane knew that very well. "I wouldn't have gone alone if someone who shall remain nameless had not pulled her covers over her head. You know Grandison cannot wait for you to feel like getting up! Did you want an accident in our chamber?" The impulse to confide in her sister faded. She would eventually tell Cassandra all, but not while she was feeling cross. And she was feeling cross because she was feeling guilty.

"I'm sorry, Jane." Cassandra hugged her, not minding that Jane still held the muddy cloth. Jane instantly felt a wretch for being in a bad mood with her sister. Their love for each other was beyond such little things. "But it was just so warm in bed. I don't have your appetite for striding across muddy fields when it's barely light."

"Oh, but it's the best time of day in a city!" said Jane, patting Grandison to signal she had concluded her clean up and peace was restored. "The world is fresh, the mist is on the water, only people with business being about are abroad. No idlers, no slugabeds."

Cassandra bowed, accepting the insult. "I'm pleased you enjoyed your walk then. I imagine you have worked up an appetite for breakfast?"

"That I have." Jane washed her hands in the scullery and followed her sister into the dining room. "What shall we do today?"

Cassandra took her place, choosing a chair in the sunshine. "Henry sent word that he has his first race at noon. If he wins this, he'll be in for the semi-final tomorrow, and after that the final!"

The breakfast room was empty, the Secretary to the Canal already at work, the Lambtons not yet risen. Jane sat beside Cassandra and helped herself to a hot roll. She slathered it with butter.

"Does that mean his water adventure ends today then?" She grinned at Cassandra.

"O ye of little faith!" Cassandra shook her head in mock disappointment. "He's an Austen: he will rise to the challenge."

"He will, but will the rest of the crew?"

To give Henry his due, his fellow oarsmen did look somewhat better prepared this morning than they had at their practice. Young Lambton was not gazing at the clouds but swinging his arms in circles to warm up, the cox was lost in a yet deeper frown, and Henry was bouncing with nervous energy. He kissed his sisters, shook hands with his father, then wrestled with Grandison.

"Bring us luck, old boy!" he implored.

"That's no way to talk to our papa," said Jane.

"I was talking to the dog, Minx." Henry sighed and glanced over at the opposition.

"Whom are you rowing against?" asked Mr Austen.

"New College." Henry sounded worried.

"Oh, if they are new, then you will have an advantage," said Cassandra, always quick to find a bright side.

"In the manner of Oxford, New College is in fact one of the oldest, and one of the biggest and richest. It was the headquarters of Charles I during the Civil War," said their father.

"And look what good that did him!" Jane cut in. "The doomed king did not benefit from the association so neither shall their boat. You'll beat them easily. We have every faith in you, Henry." There: she had done her sisterly duty. It was up to Henry to come good.

Leaving Henry to arrange his team in their places and give final words of encouragement like his namesake before the Battle of Agincourt, the three Austens and Grandison made their way downstream to find a good vantage point. In this kind of race it was not the finish line that mattered, because the pursuer could overtake the other boat it was chasing at any moment. All New College had to do was hold on in front until they reached the end point at Donnington.

"Where shall we wait?" asked Jane.

Her father eyed the opposing crew, then Henry's boat. "They shouldn't have too much trouble overhauling them. I think we would be well advised to wait here."

Jane couldn't see what her father did in the New College boat. The eight men all looked strong and lean. They were laughing and joking, either very confident they would win or not bothered about the outcome.

"Why do you say that, Papa?" Cassandra asked.

"Complacency has no place in a race." He folded his hands on the top of his walking cane. "You'll see."

They were joined by Mr Jenkinson and the Lambtons soon after.

"You're not in the team, Mr Jenkinson?" asked Cassandra once greetings had been exchanged.

"Heavens, no!" said Jenkinson, coppery hair catching the fleeting sun as it ducked out from a cloud. "My clumsiness is only magnified on the water. I go forward when the others go back and vice versa. And I can't swim."

"Then you shall join us in cheering them on. If Henry hears us, he'll try twice as hard. He won't let us down." Jane let out a practice whistle, turning many heads and making Grandison's ears prick forward.

"Good gracious, what a noise!" said Mrs Lambton, looking scandalized.

"My sons taught her," said Mr Austen apologetically. "Jane and Cassandra come from a rough and tumble house of boys, I'm afraid. They were bound not to emerge unscathed despite the best efforts of their mother. Well, perhaps Cassandra did, but Jane...?" He looked affectionately at his younger daughter.

Jane slipped her hand in his. "I won't whistle again, if you don't want me to."

"No, dear Jane, you do what you must. Who is there who knows us in this crowd?" Mr Austen gestured around to the motley selection of friends, family, and the curious who had turned out to watch the boats. "And your brother will be listening out for our support – that duty comes first."

Sometimes her father's strict moral code was of great help

against the social rules in which her mother liked to entangle her. He thought it more important to tramp through the fields to go to the bedside of a sick person, than to worry that eyebrows would be raised at the state of your hems when you got there. Cheering on Henry fell into this category.

A pistol was fired and the boats started off with a huge lunge at the oars. Jane and her party were too far away to see who had the better start, the angle all wrong to gauge if the gap was closing, but both crews had clean starts, no crabs caught, no mistimed strokes. Jenkinson sighed, probably because he envied his fellows doing something he was constitutionally unable to achieve.

"You could always try single sculling," said Jane in consolation.

As the boats approached, the college supporters, who were running down the Thames path like hounds after a fox, drew ominously nearer. Jane and her party were in danger of being mown down, as the young men weren't watching where they were going, eyes on the straining backs of their fellows, encouragements yelled at the boats. It was a stampede.

"Grandison!" said Jane, anticipating the disaster to come.

Understanding his role, the dog took up a stance in front of Cassandra and Jane as the New College men ran towards them, protecting the girls behind his canine body. The frontrunner collided with him. Grandison scampered back but the man went down, tripping the one behind, and another – and another. It was a glorious pile of New College men which was greatly cheered by the St John men who followed. Even Mr Austen seemed pleased, though he offered a hand to one of the unfortunates to help them to their feet.

"So sorry, Sir, Miss," said the abashed student, reverting from fox hound to polite young man whose manners made him welcome in society.

"Oh, don't miss the race!" called Cassandra. She had not turned her eyes away from the real drama down on the water. "Come on, Henry!"

Jane whistled.

"Austens for ever!" yelled Mr Austen.

"Pull, Michael!" called Mrs Lambton. "Pull!"

Mr Lambton joined Jane with an admirable whistle that screeched in the air like the call of a barn owl. He winked when his eyes met Jane's astonished ones.

They weren't perfectly placed to see the deciding moments of the race, but they were not far off. Henry's crew pulled for all they were worth, the cox hunkered down like some malevolent dwarf out of a German fairy tale casting maledictions on the opposition. St John's heaved, New College pulled – heave, pull, heave, pull – and then the prow of Henry's boat bumped the stern of their opponents.

"A hit! A very palpable hit!" shouted Mr Austen.

Henry glanced around, looking for them. He grinned when he saw them hurrying up the path to catch up and gave them a two-handed victory salute. He almost lost his oar but caught it just in time. That was so typical. Jane smiled. Mr Austen, Cassandra, and Jane held hands and raised them. They shouted in unison, Henry joining in:

"Austens for ever!"

Jenkinson watched them in wonder. He waited for the celebration to die down before remarking. "I thought it was just Henry, but now I am convinced the entire family is extremely…" he searched for a polite word, "unique."

Chapter 14

The celebration of the first victory lasted for the rest of the day. Jane thought that most of Henry's joy was due to his relief at not having disgraced himself before his sisters. There were still another two races to consider, but that was tomorrow's problem. Mr Austen ordered a special dinner at the Mitre, one of the chief taverns in town. They had a private room to themselves, and Henry brought Jenkinson with him as his guest. They were a merry party, playing word games and cards long after the dishes had been cleared away – all told, a very jolly holiday.

As the clocks struck eight, Mr Austen rose.

"It is time your sisters went to their room and we returned to college. We can't have the captain of the boat missing his next race because he grew overtired."

Jane looped her hand through Henry's elbow and was content for her brother to steer her safely along Cornmarket, avoiding any dark alleys where danger might be lurking.

"You didn't think I could do it, did you, Jane?" Henry asked as they approached the lodgings, a spray of stars overhead, the leaves of a great plane tree waving like many hands applauding the display. A couple drifted down like flowers thrown at a prima donna after a magnificent performance.

Jane squeezed his arm. "I may have joked about it, but deep down, I know to trust that you will do your very best. I'm so pleased for you."

He smiled. "The strange thing I'm learning here is that while we are supposed to be at Oxford for the book learning, it is the lessons we learn outside the classroom that produce the greatest ripples among the men. If I can succeed at this, it will establish me as a very fine fellow among my peers."

"We already know you are a very fine fellow," said Jane.

"Ah yes, but you are not exactly unbiased. I would like the world to know that I can command a team – and earn their respect."

"You will, Henry, you will." A little worry about the next race entered her mind. "But, as Father would say, being a gallant loser is also a noble calling."

"To which we say," whispered Henry, "fiddlesticks – winning's the thing!" They laughed, as indeed the Austen children had said this to each other in the nursery when fighting over the outcome of many a game. "I will bid you goodnight, Jane."

Just as they were about to part on the doorstep, a bell tolled from over the rooftops. It couldn't be for the hour as it was gone eight, and it did not stop. Shutters were thrown open on the upper storeys as people looked out to see if they could catch sight of flames or smoke.

"What does that mean?" asked Jane. It sounded like a warning. "Is there a fire?"

"We'd better go in and enquire," said her father. "And if there is, I don't want you on the street a moment longer."

As they made to enter, Mr Herbert hurried out, still pulling on his jacket. The Austens had to flatten themselves against the wall to make way.

"Excuse me, Sir, Miss Austen – I must dash!" he said, not giving way to the girls as manners usually dictated.

"Mr Herbert, whatever is the matter?" called Mr Austen.

The man just waved his arm over his head and ran out of view.

Mrs Hill came to the door, her cap strings askew and apron rucked up on one side as if she hadn't had time to stop and smooth it down.

"Oh, there you are – thank goodness, I was about to send my servant for you. Come in, come in, where it is safe." She hurried them into the parlour, even those who were not her guests.

"Mrs Hill, do you know what is happening?" asked Mr Austen, glancing at his daughters with concern.

"That bell? It means one of the convicts has run off. Got loose he has. Mr Herbert heard it and his face went pale as a fillet of cod." She took Cassandra's shawl from her and put it near the fire to drive out the damp it had collected from the evening air. "Seems to me he thinks it might be one of his workers. They were working late to finish that monstrosity over yonder – his orders, so I guess he is feeling bad he caused all this disturbance." She noticed her apron was awry and straightened it with forceful tugs. "Some of us said it weren't safe, having those men out from behind the walls of the gaol where they belong. Tea, Miss Austen?"

Cassandra nodded. "Thank you."

"Don't you worry, Reverend, I'll keep your girls safe. No going out without a male chaperone, you hear me?" she said to Cassandra and Jane, though her gaze was mostly on Jane as the offender in that area after her early morning ramble. "A desperate man will do desperate things. You keep yourself far away from any place he might be hiding until they catch him."

Jane thought herself hardly the sort to go throwing herself into the path of a wicked man, at least not without a good reason.

"Tea would be lovely, thank you," she said instead, to prevent Mrs Hill mentioning anything about her dog-walking habits. She had survived the day without discussing them with anyone but Cassandra and meant to keep it that way.

Dear Frank,

There is great excitement in Oxford, overshadowing even Henry's victory in his first race. What could be more important than that Austen moment of glory, you cry? Well, I'll tell you: one of the convicts working on the canal has escaped! What do you think of that? Is it not the most exciting thing you've heard since the Parisians overthrew the Bastille Prison in July? Doubtless you are now wondering how such a thing could happen. That was our question to Mr Herbert, Secretary to the Canal, when he returned from his emergency meeting with the Governor of the gaol. He believes that an accomplice had hidden a file near the water bucket, and the convict had used this to free himself from his chains as dusk approached and ran off into the night. His manacles were found abandoned by the path to the canal.

We are all on high alert, but please tell Mama there is no chance that he will come anywhere near our lodgings and we are quite safe. What I would prefer you did not mention is that I saw the miscreant while walking Grandison this morning. How thrilling this now seems! I can report that he was indeed hovering near the water bucket. I wondered why he was so hostile to me watching him there. I guess his friend had already left the file for him overnight to collect and I almost spoiled that for him. He either slipped it into his pocket when he pretended to throw the ladle at the bucket, or returned later to secure it. I wish I'd been paying more attention to his movements, but I was disconcerted by his manner. Whatever the sequence of events, he is in the wind, as the saying goes, and all are now looking for him. The hue and cry has been raised, and there will be many sleepless householders in Oxford tonight as they join the hunt.

What was his crime, you ask? That will give you some comfort, as he is not a violent man, by all

accounts, but merely one who cheated his customers.
I enclose one of the bills that have been posted around
Oxford for you to peruse and shiver at this delicious
bit of news!

Cassandra, Henry, Papa, and Grandison send their
love.

Yours affectionately,

Jane

P.S. Henry's boat trounced New College, which is
apparently old, but he handed them the new experience
of being beaten by the even newer men.

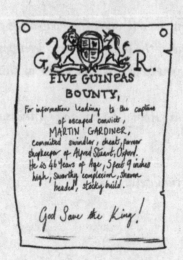

Chapter 15

After the excitement of the night before, Jane woke with the feeling that it would be wrong to be spending the day doing something so frivolous as watching college students rowing. Not that she could think what she might do to assist in the hunt for Gardiner. She could offer to lend Grandison, who had a nose worthy of a bloodhound, but her father had said the authorities were well furnished with their own dogs. Indeed, they were already out in the meadows by the canal and river, and he was confident it wouldn't be long before the man was found.

She strolled with her father towards the Thames. They kept close to the college walls to avoid splashes from the carriages rumbling along cobbled streets. Jane had spent most of her life in the countryside and so cities always struck her as dirty places, much more so than the honest mud of a village like Steventon. There she knew what went into the mire – you only had to watch the rain fall and see the herds of animals pass to make a shrewd guess. Here some puddles had an oily sheen, and the stench in alleyways was stomach churning.

Best not to think too much about it if she wanted to keep her breakfast down. She distracted herself by watching her sister. Cassandra was walking ahead with Jenkinson, her hand resting in the crook of the student's arm. Jane decided that her sister and Jenkinson made a pretty picture: Cassandra in her pink day gown and sky-blue pelisse and Jenkinson in a smart green jacket and buckskin breeches. Even better was that her sister was in no danger of falling in love with the shy scholar and so could converse rationally and show how intelligent she was. Henry's friend too had lost some of his bashfulness in their company and proved capable of conversation unseeded with his studied compliments.

"Has anyone told the narrowboat people that they might be in danger?" Jane asked her father as they passed a wagon heading for the excavation.

"I imagine that is in hand," said her father, not sounding too worried.

"Hmm, I wonder." Jane remembered how Georgie had described the gulf between the locals and the canal people. She could well imagine that the boat owners would be last on the list of people to be told if there was trouble abroad – which was an oversight on the part of the authorities, because what better way for a convict to escape than hidden, say, in the cargo hold of a canal boat? The storage holds were dark, often full of coal. It would be easy for someone to cover themselves in the dust and be very well camouflaged. That was what she would do if she were on the run. She had given it some thought last night when she had finished her letter to Frank.

Her silence pricked her father's suspicions.

"Jane?" he said warily. "You aren't thinking of getting involved, are you?" He knew his youngest daughter well.

"This escape is none of your business. I would counsel you to leave well alone. You mustn't even think any more about it."

"I won't get involved in the hunt – obviously not," said Jane quickly. "I'm not so foolish, Papa." She had considered – and rejected – that already. "But I made friends with a girl on one of the barges yesterday—"

"You did? When did you get time to do that?" Her father frowned, his mutton-chop whiskers bristling.

"Um, when I walked Grandison?" Jane was a truthful girl. She might not tell her father everything, but she wouldn't lie either when asked a direct question. "It was early. There was no one around, well, apart from the canal people. They work so hard. Up at dawn to start moving. Isn't that admirable?"

Her attempts to divert her father onto a discussion of the virtues of hard workers failed. "You are to do no such thing again. At least you had your sister with you for decency's sake, but this escape means that no young lady can be abroad early or late without protection of a father or an older brother."

Jane opened her mouth to confess that she had gone alone but Mr Austen sailed on.

"I shudder when I remember that it was I myself and Henry that took you into the company of such wastrels but two days ago! I knew it was wrong at the time, but my desire to offer a spiritual word of comfort got the better of my common sense." He shook his head at the memory of his rashness. "Please forgive my indiscretion. I hope you and Cassandra were not too upset by being forced into such low company?"

Jane closed her mouth, reconsidered, then said:

"No need to apologize, Papa, especially not to me. You know I find everything of interest and I understood perfectly the impulse that took you over to speak to them." He didn't look convinced so more was needed. "Dear Papa, Cassandra and I both appreciate that you do not hide us from those who deserve our compassion – and who is more deserving than the prisoner among us, one of God's lost sheep? We were never in any danger."

He patted her hand and smiled, his conscience lightened by her words. Jane's, however, was burdened, as she had not told her father that she had sought out the convicts a second time – and on her own, with only her dog for company. It was imprudent now she thought about it, but it was so hard not to be curious! Life offered such a fascinating bundle of twigs from which she could weave her own nest of stories. Imagining life from the point of view of such a man as Gardiner was one exceedingly useful sprig indeed.

The competition was progressing very satisfactorily for St John's. Henry's team made short work of the Magdalen boat, thanks to the opposition team turning up a man down. No one could find the missing teammate, and it was rumoured he'd taken a sudden invitation from a young lord to attend a house party on a great estate and abandoned Oxford for a few days. The rich danced to their own tune, Henry grumbled. Magdalen had elected to go ahead with the race but were overtaken before they had even got out of sight of the boathouses. It was a little anticlimactic compared with the thrilling race of the day before.

"Your brother might actually do it: he might actually win this little competition," said Mr Austen merrily as they waited for the boats to row back to the start line. The final was due to take place as soon as the St John's team had had a chance to rest, which meant that the Austens elected to stay in their positions on the bank. "Good old St John's!"

"You sound as though you doubted their chances," said Jane, plucking a blade of grass and stripping the seeds from the head to make a little bouquet between finger and thumb.

"'Doubt' might be too strong a word." Mr Austen looked sheepish. "But we were never distinguished as a college by our exploits on the river in my day. And please do not say anything to Henry."

Jane smiled and threw the seeds into the air. She watched them stream away on the breeze. The same wind tugged on her bonnet strings and Cassandra's muslin skirts. Everything was in movement as the river rolled by on its way to London and eventually out to sea. Willows rippled and lashed, yellowed leaves losing their grip and joining the grass seeds as they tumbled and twisted away. How short was the stay of living things! Holding seeds here one day, then they'd be buried in the earth the next. In spring they would each be their own grass stalks, bearing their own seeds – and so on and on in an endless chain, perhaps to be plucked by another girl like Jane in the future? This moment sitting here with her father, thinking of Henry's chances, watching the boats on the water – that too would soon be distant, maybe even forgotten… unless she wrote it down.

She wished she had brought a pen.

"I think they are ready at last!" said Cassandra, jumping to her feet.

"I believe you are right, Miss Austen," said Jenkinson, helping her to stand on a tree stump that was her chosen vantage point for the race.

"Oh, I do hope he wins," said Cassandra, clasping her hands to her heart.

"Never doubt it, my dear," said their father, with a wink at Jane.

It was time. Jane got up on the fallen branch of a willow tree that had given up the effort of keeping its boughs aloft.

The two boats rowed to the starting line, Henry's face bright with the excitement of pitting his team against their rival college, Christchurch. To win would bring fame in the halls of St John's; to lose would bring shame that he would have to bear for the rest of his university career – and possibly beyond! Agitated for him, Jane clutched her skirts, squeezing the muslin in her fingers, crushing the material beyond hope of uncreasing before the next wash.

"Please do win, Henry!" she murmured.

The starting pistol cracked the air.

But then, just as the gunshot still echoed and the rowers heaved into their first stroke, shrill whistles sounded, urgent, fearful, the kind used to summon the watch or the firemen's wagon. The crowd looked about them in confusion.

"What's going on?" Jane asked, but none in her party had any clue.

Oblivious, the St John's crew pulled hard, oars dipping in unison, intent on their quarry.

Out of the nearest field fringing the Thames, a man in muddy rags burst through the willow branches, almost at her feet. Jane squeaked: he was like a grouse startled by the beaters. He looked behind him, hesitated, then ran *towards* the boat race. In a flash, Jane realized that it was the convict! The thunder of hooves signalled the onset of the militia at his heels. Gardiner had been spotted! They were witnessing the end of the hunt.

"There he is!" cried the chief hunter, an officer with a black beard and scarlet coat, waving a sabre above his head. He wheeled his horse around and directed its course down the path on which the spectators were clustered. "Make way! In the name of the king!"

The people shrieked and scrambled to get off the narrow passage along the riverbank. There weren't many places to go. The boats in their fierce competition rowing one way were forgotten as men, women, and children scattered like startled ducks before the horses galloping towards them. Gardiner, now his hideout in the fields had been discovered, calculated that his best chance of escape was to go among the people. The militia could hardly ride down the good folk of Oxford. He wove and ducked between the spectators, choosing a path between the old men, women, and children, avoiding anyone who looked like they might tackle him. As he dodged, Jane's gaze met his briefly as she stood raised above the crowd on her branch. His eyes were bloodshot, face sweaty, arms flailing wildly to make a passage through – a desperate creature who would bite if any dared reach out to him. He scared her deeply – something she only now acknowledged when she was out of his reach.

Mr Lambton showed more courage than most and tried to step in his way. Gardiner's answer was to shove the obstacle into the river, and Mr Lambton landed with a great splash. He came up spluttering, his hat floating away like a toy boat.

"Oh, Mr Lambton!" shrieked his wife as she tottered on the edge herself.

Jane leaped from the branch and grabbed Mrs Lambton's arm to pull her to safety. Mr Austen swept Jane and Mrs Lambton back behind his body, cramming them against the hedge, as Jenkinson stood in front of Cassandra. Gardiner rammed past, forcing another man into the Thames.

Oh dear: she couldn't see anything now! But she had to do something or he'd get away. Jane reached down and slipped the leash from Grandison's neck.

"Go get him!" she urged.

With a happy woof, Grandison shot like a bolt from a crossbow, outpacing the horsemen and easily catching up with the convict as he leapt up the steps to town. But rather than lay his teeth into the man's jacket and bring him to the ground as Jane had intended, Grandison danced along at his side, looking for all the world like he intended to follow him on this wonderful game of chase.

Mr Lambton was hauled to the shore and his wife patted him dry ineffectually with her handkerchief, her breaths coming in broken sobs.

"Jane!" said her father. "What were you thinking?"

"Well, that didn't quite go to plan," she admitted. "Grandison, come back!"

But too late: her dog had run off with the escaped convict like the dish with the spoon in the nursery rhyme and disappeared with him into the alleyways of the city. Last she heard was a happy bark that became a howl.

"Grandison!" Jane gulped, tears pricking her eyes. "He'll come back," she said hoarsely.

"If he's allowed," her father said grimly. "Your mother said that you needed a lesson in prudence, but I wish you had not chosen to learn it at the expense of so beloved a pet." Seeing her misery, he folded her to his chest. "There, there, Jane dear. You did well saving Mrs Lambton a dousing. And it would be a very wicked man indeed to harm that foolish dog. We'll post a reward for Grandison's safe return. I'm sure someone will find your dog, if he doesn't find us first."

Safe in his embrace, Jane nodded. She vowed she would never give in to such bold impulses ever again. Rational and calm were to be her goals in life from henceforward, if only Grandison returned safely.

Naturally, the race had been called off as soon as people ended up in the water. All were rescued by the rowers with the only fatal casualty being Mr Lambton's hat.

Back in St John's, Henry announced to the company that he was annoyed that he had missed the fun on the bank.

"Fun!" growled their father. They were taking tea in Henry's room. The room was steamily hot with many visitors, a roaring fire, and a kettle bubbling on the grate. An enticing smell of buttered toast rose up as an offering to the lion on the college crest carved into the mantlepiece. Two students had taken on the task of making some for the company, slicing the white loaf in generous wedges, pronging them on a fork, and dancing the slices over the flames to get an even browning. Once done to their satisfaction, they buttered them, slapped on some jam, and passed it to the nearest taker. Jane was for once happy with the practice of "ladies first", meaning she and Cassandra were served with early slices; else she feared she would never have seen a crumb before a young man, with an appetite sharpened by exercise, gulped it down well in advance of it reaching her. Henry's friends were like seagulls watching the arrival of the fishing fleet, quick to spot an opportunity to feed.

Jenkinson had just finished a spirited account of the altercation to the impressed teammates. They had only caught glimpses from where they sat on the water in their boat. Michael Lambton was among them, sharing Henry's importance as his family also had been caught up in the debacle, and his father among those nobly rescued from the Thames. The young men declared Lambton senior a top fellow for risking his neck and much praised him for his bravery. Unfortunately, Mrs Lambton's nerves had suffered a shock at seeing her husband propelled into the Thames, and so Michael's parents had retired to their lodgings to recover. That meant they were not present to hear the praises sung.

"You young men," continued Mr Austen, "have an odd idea about fun. I can't see anything fun about people being dunked like linens on washday and the rest of us being forced into the hedge!"

"Well, obviously not fun when you almost got squashed by the cavalry!" Henry's eyes glowed with typical Austen delight in anything out of the ordinary. His friends tried to look suitably quelled, but none of them were doing a very good job. "But to see the fugitive so close – and to have our dog involved in the hunt – what a tale I will have to tell at dinner tonight!"

"Hear, hear!" muttered his friends.

"Dinner?" Mr Austen arched his brow. "Henry, we won't be sitting down to dinner until Grandison is safely restored to us." Mr Austen had dispatched Benjamin around town to post reward notices, but so far no one had come forward with the dog. Jane was losing confidence that Grandison would be back soon. He liked adventures, and he might not have the sense to know that this was a very dangerous one.

"I do hope Miss Jane is not too despondent?" said one teammate, sending Jane a commiserating smile.

"Take heart, Miss, your hound will return," said another. "My spaniel often goes astray chasing rabbits on my estate, but she always finds her way home – eventually."

She gave Henry's friends a teary smile.

"I hope he bites that cad!" said Michael, waving his buttered toast in the air. "My father could've drowned!"

Unlikely, as there were many people on hand, thought Jane.

Cassandra squeezed Jane's shoulder. "Mr Lambton, I think we should hope Grandison doesn't provoke the man. Gardiner must be desperate and, as our landlady said, desperate men do desperate things."

Jane cleared her throat and blinked back her tears. She was an Austen, not a watering can! "Happily, Grandison is a friendly soul," she said stoutly. "He is unlikely to bite anyone, even a wicked man like Gardiner, so I will choose to believe he will be returned safe and sound."

"Indeed, Jane, that is the best way to look at things," said Mr Austen, getting to his feet. "And if you don't mind, gentlemen, I think my daughters have had quite enough excitement for one day and should return to their lodgings."

This announcement brought many offers from the young men of a gallant escort across the road. Mr Austen picked Jenkinson and Lambton, while he and Henry went to the senior fellows of the college to describe why the expected boat race triumph had had to be deferred.

As Jane and Cassandra crossed the road with their two new friends, Benjamin the porter's boy wove through the traffic towards them. He took off his cap and waved it in the air.

"Miss Jane! Miss Jane!"

A cart piled with hay passed, momentarily blocking him from their view.

He popped out from underneath like a hare in a cornfield. "Come quickly! I spotted him – I spotted Grandison!"

Chapter 16

"You have?" Jane could have danced for pure relief. Never had a freckled nose and two bright eyes in a round face been such a welcome sight! "Where?"

Benjamin put his cap back on and touched the brim to the two students, suddenly shy in front of the young gentlemen.

"Speak up, Ben," said Lambton kindly. "Don't keep the young ladies in suspense."

"I'm not sure, sir," Benjamin said, looking sheepish now, "but I think I saw Miss Jane's dog as I crossed the canal on my way back from posting the notices."

"Really?" squeaked Jane. This at least seemed confirmation that nothing terrible had happened to Grandison.

"Yes, Miss. He was down on the towpath, and it were a bit misty so I wasn't certain – but I think he was trotting along as cool as the proverbial cucumber, looking as if he had a fair mind to go all the way to Wolvercote village. He didn't appear to know he was lost."

That sounded like Grandison. He took the world as he found it, always at home.

"Oh, why didn't you go down and get him?" asked Jane. *So close!* The danger was that he would be long gone by the time they went back for him.

Ben fumbled the remaining notices for Grandison's recapture that he still carried in his pocket. "Sorry, Miss, but you see he were too far away. He didn't hear when I called."

"I see." Jane thought it more likely her dog had chosen to ignore. Grandison had selective hearing.

Benjamin rubbed his sleeve across his brow, his face shiny with all the running around town he had been doing. He shot a look at Jenkinson. "He seemed to have a destination in mind though. He wasn't sniffing like most dogs do, you know, in and out of the bushes? I thought I'd best come back and tell you as he's more likely to come to you than me."

That was true enough. She had to get back to the canal.

"Mr Jenkinson—" began Jane.

The young man held up a hand. "Miss Jane, I promised your father faithfully that I would deliver you and your sister to your lodgings with no detours."

Jane smiled sweetly at him and pointed to the door. "And that you have. We have arrived. Now we have to go out again."

"Very good logic," he said approvingly, "but unfortunately I am aware of the spirit of my agreement as well as the letter. That does not include gallivanting off on unauthorized missions on the vague possibility that Grandison was the same dog as the one spotted on the towpath. However," he glanced at Lambton and got a nod, "Lambton and I will undertake to search for your dog ourselves, with Ben's help. I'm sure the three of us can find him between us – if he's still there to be found."

Benjamin did not look too sure, chewing on his bottom lip. He was probably worrying about the escaped convict being close by.

"Capital idea, Jenks," said Lambton. "We wouldn't want the ladies out and about until the scoundrel is found. Please go on inside, Miss Austen, Miss Jane, and we'll set off at once."

There was no polite way to refuse – not without a most unflattering report going directly back to her father, then by letter to her mother, and bringing the most terrible consequences down on her head. Jane might've risked it for herself, but not when it also involved Cassandra.

"You will bring me word directly?" she asked, dragging her heels as she walked backwards into the house.

"We either return with your dog or a clear report that it is a case of mistaken identity," vowed Jenkinson.

That would have to do. "Very well."

"And thank you," said Cassandra, nudging Jane, "for going to all this trouble for us. We really do appreciate it." She gave Jane a look to remind her that her manner came across as less than appreciative.

Jane recognized the justice of the reproof. "Yes, thank you. I apologize if I do not sound grateful; I'm just so worried about Grandison."

Jenkinson saluted her like a soldier going off into battle on the orders of his general. "Then let us find your dog and bring an end to your anxiety."

Seeing the Austen sisters safely in the hallway, he closed the door behind them and headed off with Benjamin and Lambton.

"I hate being a girl sometimes," sighed Jane. "I want to do something!"

"You can't change the world, Jane. We have to find our own ways to manage such trials. You might take it as a lesson in patience." Cassandra had always been more philosophical about the constraints of being born female.

"They won't find him, will they?" said Jane morosely.

"They might." Cassandra took her sister by the arm and propelled her upstairs. "There's nothing you can do tonight."

The three searchers returned empty-handed. Jane was not surprised. Only Benjamin had had any chance of catching Grandison when he had first spotted him, and he had muffed it. She couldn't say that though, as it would have been rude and would make the boy feel bad; instead, she had to thank them for their efforts.

"He'll turn up," said Jenkinson, not looking convinced.

"We'll see," said Jane wearily.

Even though Cassandra had managed to fall asleep up in their attic bedroom, Jane could not. The moon floated above the college turrets and treetops, untouched by all the events of the day. By contrast, Jane felt like a feverish mess of worry and confusion. Why had Grandison gone off like that? Perhaps he was not the world's cleverest dog, but surely he must've understood she hadn't meant to send him away for so long? He knew where they were staying, or at least could sniff his way back.

But maybe he had decided it was time to go home? His reasoning processes were his own and followed a doggy rather than human logic.

She had a sudden terrible vision of him taking it into his head to go home – to his real home. Was he even now trotting unconcernedly down the turnpike road heading south? He'd be knocked over by the mail coach, or stolen by travellers, or shot by a farmer...

Her imagination was relentless, throwing up all sorts of scenarios. The possibilities got grimmer and grimmer. No! This was not to be borne! Jane threw back the covers. There was one thing she could do and should have done earlier when she first thought of it.

Taking out pen and ink, she wrote her note. She took care to print rather than use her usual elegant hand, as it was possible that Georgie had not had much time to learn to read. Perhaps her father would read it to her if not?

Dear Georgie,

I hope you do not mind that I am writing to you, but after our conversation this morning, I felt that we might be on the way to being friends. As your friend, I have three grave pieces of news to tell you, and I cannot be confident that anyone here has thought to keep you and your father informed of the great doings in the city.

First, you should know that one of the convicts has escaped! He goes by the name of Gardiner and is by all accounts a bad lot who cheated his customers. He is a big man with powerful hands, dressed in ragged grey, with flashing brown eyes, every inch the ne'er-do-well. He ran off a day ago and is being sought for a reward. You might have heard the rumours by this time and seen the search parties;

now you know the cause. Your father might wish to check the villain is not hiding somewhere among your cargo, and he should pass the word to other boatmen to watch out for him. I do not know if Gardiner is a violent man, but he is desperate, which might be enough to drive him to do bad things.

The second piece of news is unfortunately connected. I was caught up earlier today in the hunt for the convict. We were watching a boat race and Gardiner broke from cover in the river meadows. As he ran past, I sent Grandison to chase him down, but my dog – foolish, foolish hound! – chose to tag along after him instead. Grandison cannot judge between friend and foe and misunderstood his errand. I fear the convict has kept him, perhaps for protection, perhaps because he fears the dog will give away his location. My last piece of news is that Grandison might have been spotted this evening near where you met us this morning, which suggests the possibility that Grandison led the man to the canal, a place my dog likes very much. He might even bring him to your doorstep. If you see Grandison, or the convict, please let me know at the above address.

Yours in haste,

Jane Austen

No matter how she bent her arguments, Jane couldn't justify going out herself to deliver the message – her father would be incensed and pack her off home, her mother would lock her in her bedroom until she was twenty-five, and Cassandra would probably not speak to her for a month! Instead, she went down into the kitchen and begged a favour from the scullery maid, with the reward of a penny. The girl in question was happy enough to take the message, as she went out at dawn to fetch the milk from the dairy and Georgie's boat wasn't far out of her way.

"Besides, Miss," the girl said with a grin, "I always had a fancy to see one of 'em boats. So pretty and neat they be, like little cottages, curtains and stove, very comfortable. Not so much work keeping one of 'em shipshape. Maybe I could stow away one day?"

Jane agreed that a narrowboat was a most rational way of living and returned upstairs to her bed. The message would be delivered at dawn. She had to hope the next day would bring her better news.

Chapter 17

A note sat by Jane's plate at breakfast. The handwriting was painstaking but perfectly legible.

> *MISS JANE*

It had been folded into the shape of a paper boat, which was clue enough as to who was writing to her. Checking she was not observed by the Lambtons or Mr Herbert, who were buttering their muffins and lamenting the lack of progress in the hunt for the convict, Jane unfolded the paper. Cassandra watched her carefully but did not give her away. Jane had already confessed about the early-morning note.

Just as Jane had hoped, it was an answer to her own letter. Georgie had used the back of a leaflet for a Methodist preaching meeting in Coventry, showing she had picked up an education somewhere on the canal, either from her father or perhaps at Sunday school. This was where most poor children in Steventon had a chance to learn their letters, as they had to work on the farms during the week.

TO MISS JANE

THANK YOU FOR YOUR LETTER. DAD SAYS NO
PRISNER IN OUR COAL HOLE BUT HE WILL
PASS THE WORD ALONG.

SORRY ABOUT YOUR DOG. DAD SAYS THE
ARMY ARE OUT AND ARE QUICK TO SHOOT.
YOU HAD BEST FIND GRANSON BEFORE
THEY DO.

WE KNOW GOOD PLACES TO HIDE UP THE
CANAL. I WILL SHOW YOU. TELL YOUR DAD
WE GO FOR A TRIP UP TO THE DOOK'S CUT
TODAY. MANY FINE VISITORS GO THERE. IF
WE FIND GRANSON, WE CAN RESCUE HIM
AND TELL THE OFFICERS WHERE TO FIND
THE PRISNER.

DAD GIVES HIS WORD YOU WILL BE
SAFE. CANAL PEOPLE LOOK AFTER EACH
OTHER. WE DO NOT FEAR THE CHEATING
SHOPKEEPER.

YOURS

GEORGINA CARTER

Jane passed the note to Cassandra. "What do you think? Is there any chance Papa will let us go?"

"He might." Cassandra slipped the note into her pocket. "But only if we take Henry. Papa is eager to go to Oxford Prison today and offer spiritual guidance to the Governor at this difficult time."

"How did that come about?" Jane selected a boiled egg from the warming dish and set it in a little blue and white eggcup. "Doesn't he have his own chaplain – for the prison?"

"It turns out the Governor and Papa are old acquaintances from Papa's time in Oxford. After our visit to the basin, Papa's interest was rekindled, and he also wants to counsel any inmates who wish to speak to a man of the cloth." Cassandra dipped the end of a crust into her soft-boiled egg. "He wants to help quieten the excitement that follows after someone escapes."

Jane gave her a quizzical look.

"Think of it like startled sheep fleeing the pen. One escape might lead to others trying unless they can be calmed down. He'll be grateful that we are safely out of the way."

Mr Herbert had clearly heard her last remarks during a lull in his own conversation because he grimaced at the suggestion of further escapes. "Another muffin, Miss Austen?"

"Thank you." Cassandra took a bun from under the napkin that kept them warm. Jane tapped her egg and peeled off the bits of shell.

"What's this about your father attending the gaol?" Mr Herbert's tone was overly casual, which usually meant he was hiding his real interest. Jane frowned. The man really shouldn't be listening in on the conversation of others or, if he did, should have more tact than to betray it.

"Our father has a heart for the prisoners in our midst," said Cassandra. "As it says in the Bible, 'I was sick, and ye visited me: I was in prison, and ye came unto me.'"

Mr Herbert nodded in a patronizing way, like Cassandra was a parrot who had produced a good trick of mimicry. "Ah. Romans."

"Actually, it's from the Gospel of Matthew," said Jane.

"That's what I meant." Mr Herbert moved the basket of muffins further away so Jane couldn't reach them. He did it with an unstudied air, but she suspected it was a punishment. She stole half of Cassandra's instead, as Mr Herbert was not irritated by her sister and would keep the supply of muffins flowing in her direction.

Mr Herbert cleared his throat. "As Secretary to the Canal, I don't think it wise for your father to get involved in affairs so far away from his parish. Do you not agree, Mr Lambton? I'm not sure his bishop would approve."

What had being a secretary to do with anything? wondered Jane. His little position of power had gone to his head.

"Oh, I really cannot say—" Mr Lambton blinked like a nocturnal creature dragged into daylight.

Cassandra smiled calmly. "But, Mr Herbert, our father lived in Oxford for many years, took holy orders here, and feels responsible for all souls that he meets, not just those in his village."

"But does it not also say that charity begins at home?" Mr Herbert gave a nod to Mr and Mrs Lambton as if expecting their approval for his apposite quotation.

"That's not from the Bible." Jane dipped her teaspoon into the runny yoke of her egg.

"Oh, I'm sure it is." Mr Herbert gave her a thin-lipped smile.

"No, it is not."

Mrs Lambton fluttered her handkerchief as if Jane's words had embarrassed her. "My dear, Mr Herbert is an educated man and you a young lady of all of thirteen." Mrs Lambton's soft words implied that Jane, a mere girl, should never dare to claim any superior knowledge.

"But he's not right!"

Cassandra stepped in to calm waters. "My sister is speaking truthfully, sir, though yours is an easy assumption to make as the saying is so widespread."

"Indeed," said Mr Herbert gruffly.

"Sir Thomas Browne was the one to coin the phrase," said Jane helpfully. "My father has his books and admires his writing. I say this only so you don't make the same mistake in future. I hate it when I misquote things – which I do. Occasionally."

Mr Herbert looked at the Lambtons and raised his brows. Mrs Lambton was again prompted to come to his defence.

"Dear Jane, it is not seemly for a girl to parade her learning. You can be too clever for your own good."

"Can I?" Jane thought that a very illogical statement. "Do you mean that I should aim to be stupid and not remember what I read? Appear to be empty like this eggshell here?" She gestured to her hollowed-out boiled egg.

"Thank goodness we had boys," muttered Mr Lambton.

"Jane," murmured Cassandra. "The Duke's Cut?"

Jane recalled that her aim for the day was to get permission to take a trip up the canal. If a report of poor behaviour at breakfast reached Papa, she could wave that goodbye.

"Thank you, Mrs Lambton, your advice is very helpful." Jane pushed away the empty egg and spooned raspberry jam onto her muffin. "I have read something similar in Reverend Fordyce's *Sermons*, about good behaviour and girls appearing ignorant." She arranged her lips in a smile as sweet as the jam.

"A very good work by a worthy man," said Mrs Lambton, satisfied that Jane's education included some suitably quelling tomes. If she knew they also read radical plays and novels then she would throw up her hands and run from the room.

Papa believed that girls as well as boys were perfectly capable of making up their own minds about what they read. Jane had. Fordyce was a bore and clearly never tried living as a girl. Mr Herbert appeared to be cut from the same cloth.

"A canal boat trip?" mused Mr Austen as they strolled around St John's quad, a busy place that morning as students ran out for their lectures, and messengers came and went. Two crows strutted side-by-side on the lawn in the centre, like little avian professors in learned conversation. "I must say that does sound very amusing." He looked tempted to join his family. "Unfortunately, I am engaged for the day with Governor Harris at the prison. Might we delay it a day or two?"

No! wailed Jane silently.

Fortunately, her sister was on her side. Cassandra turned her big eyes up to him. "But Papa, we cannot stay penned in our room. Jane frets terribly for Grandison. It is far better for her to be out in the changing scenery than paint dire scenes from her imagination as to his fate."

"Indeed, indeed." Mr Austen patted Jane's hand. "I'm very sorry we have not heard news of your dog. I truly thought someone would have claimed the reward by now. He has no pedigree to make him worth stealing."

"Papa, why don't I take my sisters?" asked Henry. Cassandra had already prepared him for his part in this negotiation, and he chose his moment well – before Jane could take exception to her father's estimate of Grandison's worth. "I would welcome the fresh air and a chance to see the works up at the Duke's Cut. Another excellent feat of engineering, they say."

"Don't you have your studies?" Mr Austen paused to tell the time by the wall-mounted sundial and compare it with his pocket watch. The creeper on the wall was turning a vibrant red, leaves dropping to the flagstones.

Henry shrugged. "Jenkinson can take notes for me at the lecture. His are much better than mine in any case."

"What about your rowing?"

"They've postponed it a few days. I do not have to be back on the river until the day after tomorrow. See, I'm at a loose end." Henry spun his scholar's cap by the tassel to illustrate.

"Humph! You shouldn't be. In my day, we kept our nose to the grindstone, I can tell you. There should always be reading for you to do – more work than you can hope to get to in a term."

Jane doubted that very much. Her father liked to think he had been hard-working, but he had enough tales of college japes to suggest he had been about as diligent as Henry, which was to say, eminently distractible if a party of pleasure were in the making.

"But a family visit is cause for a holiday," argued Henry. "My tutors will understand."

Mr Austen sighed. "Very well. But you will all stay on the

boat or canal path. Any sign of danger, Henry, and I expect you to take your sisters to safety. And no falling in, Jane!"

Jane thought that she would have to be very foolish to fall in from a canal boat as there were no waves to make the vessel do more than glide, but she agreed without argument. Anything to be able to make her own search for Grandison. Cassandra was right to suggest that, if Jane had to stay in her chamber, she would drive herself wild with her imaginings.

As it was not far out of their way, they walked with Mr Austen to the gate of the prison. Like the colleges, the gaol looked like a castle – which was factually correct, as it had the distinction of being built on the site of a medieval one with a single old tower remaining just beyond the walls. The entrance and enclosure were recently rebuilt, said Mr Austen, thanks to the Governor. The buildings had fallen into a ruinous state over the centuries, but the enterprising Mr Harris had designed modifications and used the convicts to construct many parts of it. Instead of tiny rooms with no windows, no straw, no blankets, and many prisoners crammed together, now at least the inmates had a modern house of correction and a yard to walk in.

"Well, it's not paradise," said Mr Austen, "but it's a big step up from the squalor in the prison that I remember from my youth."

The gate opened to his knock and swallowed the upright figure of their father in his clerical black suit and shallow-brimmed hat. As he passed through, Jane glimpsed the women prisoners sitting in the sunshine, picking apart old ropes so that the oakum could be used for packing joints in ships to keep them watertight. It was difficult work, but it might well one day save the lives of the seamen onboard a leaking ship. A few children scrambled on the walls further off, their happy cries a contrast to the grim place in which they played. Mr Austen was already digging in his jacket pocket for the twist of barley sugars he kept there for parish children.

"The yard seems very full," said Henry. "I hear they might start sending prisoners to that new country in the southern ocean – New Holland." He offered his sisters his arms as he escorted them away. "Imagine that journey! Thousands and thousands of miles and no chance of return."

"That sounds cruel," said Jane.

Henry squeezed her hand consolingly. "Better than execution – and prisons weren't built to hold people for years at a time, just until their sentence is passed."

Jane shuddered. No, it would be unbearable to be stuck inside a place like that for life. Maybe transportation was better?

"When I was born," Henry continued, "prisoners used to be sent to the Colonies, but that has stopped since the Americans broke away from us."

As they walked, Jane felt the shadow of the prison leaving her, and she turned her face up to enjoy the autumnal sunshine.

"Were those children prisoners too?" asked Cassandra.

Henry held open the gate to the canal path for them. "I imagine some belong to those who have been imprisoned for debt and have nowhere else to go. And some will be convicted of crimes – theft usually. Age is not much of a defence. Nor poverty."

"It's not fair," said Jane. She jumped up on the gate and rode it until it closed.

Henry humoured her game with no reproof for unladylike behaviour. "No, it's not. That's why Father thinks visiting them a better use of his time today than coming on this little excursion with us." Jane sprang down and he tugged her along the path at a brisk pace. "Come, enough of the sad faces! Where is our mighty craft?"

Henry was right: they should not spoil a beautiful morning because others couldn't enjoy it with them. "It's down here," said Jane, feeling quite an old hand at the canal now she had been there several times.

They passed several narrowboats moored on the bank, stoves steaming and crockery clattering inside. Fried eggs scented the air. They attracted cheerful "how do's?" from the captains taking their ease with their pipes. Henry tapped his brim in response.

"I hope they haven't moved their boat," said Cassandra.

Jane hadn't thought of that. But Georgie would've said, surely? Unless she was playing a trick on her…?

But the *Mary-Ann* was where she had been yesterday. Nettlebed had had his mane brushed and a new ribbon put on his harness in expectation of company. Mr Carter, Georgie's father, was waiting for them.

"Mr Austen, young ladies, welcome aboard," he said, holding out a hand to assist Cassandra. Jane followed, nimble as a squirrel on the short plank. The area at the back of the boat where the rudder was located only had space for three at the most, so it was a little squashed.

Georgie came out of the cabin, throwing back the doors and releasing Rag-N'-Bone. The little dog twirled cartwheels of barking joy to see them. Georgie tried ineffectually to hush him. Jane was taken aback to see the boat girl was wearing a dress. Georgie grinned at Jane, delighted to have surprised her.

"My daughter, Georgina," said Carter, making the introduction again, as the first one Henry and Cassandra had witnessed had not been auspicious, coming at the tail end of a row between Jane and Georgie.

"Miss Carter, thank you for inviting us today," said Henry.

Georgie dipped a curtsey and blushed. Jane guessed that she might feel at her ease with a girl her own age, but not so the striking young gentleman scholar. Henry was from a higher class who rarely deigned to talk to working people like Georgie and her father. Hopefully, they would soon find the Austens were different to most of their class.

"Who wants to walk with Nettlebed and me?" Georgie asked to break the awkward moment.

"I will." Jane hopped after her to the shore and held the halter as Georgie untied the mooring ropes.

"Give him a click of the tongue and he'll start," the girl said, slapping the patient horse on the rump.

Used to this over many mornings, Nettlebed began his measured plod along the canal bank. Jane looked back over the long, low roof of the cargo hold to the little cabin and then to her brother and sister standing with Mr Carter at the stern. Henry had his hand on the rudder and was taking instruction.

"A dress?" asked Jane. She couldn't help herself.

Georgie's blue eyes twinkled. "Why not? Breeches are practical, but you're gentry. Dad said I was to look my best."

Jane secretly thought the breeches looked the best. "It's a very pretty gown." It was a faded red with white flowers embroidered along the bodice, hem, and sleeves.

"Made for me by my auntie from one of my mum's old ones."

"Your auntie? Is she on the canal too?"

"No, she has a farm over Banbury way. She makes me lots of pretty things. I think she's hoping I'll go live with her and become a decent ordinary girl." Georgie chuckled. Jane deduced that the poor auntie was going to have to come up with a better lure if she wanted to entice Georgie away from this life.

Nettlebed tossed his head and flicked his ears. He hoisted his tail to leave his calling card on the towpath. Doubtless some local would be out with a shovel to the benefit of their roses.

"How far to the Duke's Cut – and what is it?" asked Jane.

"You don't know?" Georgie shook her head in pity at Jane's ignorance. "Half a tick." She bent to rearrange the towrope.

"How do?" called an approaching bargeman.

Henry steered the *Mary-Ann* away from the bank while Mr Carter lifted the towrope over the other vessel, aided by the owner. Nettlebed stepped away from the edge so Georgie could pass the rope over the other horse. The whole movement was done so smoothly neither barge lost any speed. Georgie nodded to the boy holding the halter.

"Any news?" she asked.

The boy looked at Jane with amusement, then back at Georgie. "Lots of soldiers about. Oh, and I heard the *Mary-Ann* has taken on some toffs as deckhands."

Georgie cackled. "Aye. Bit short-handed we were."

He laughed and carried on walking.

"Who was that?" asked Jane, not in the least put out that she was being made fun of. It was so exciting to find a world within the world of England that she knew nothing about.

Georgie shrugged. "Goes by the name of Timmy Wren. That's his cousin's boat. Word is he chose this rather than become a ploughboy. He's all right."

They walked on for a few more paces, ducking as they went under the low curved archway of a brick bridge. Water cast rippling lights on the ceiling.

"It's like a cavern!" said Jane. Her voice echoed pleasingly.

Georgie gave a hoot so they could hear the reverberation. "This is nothing. There are tunnels where you have to leg it for miles."

"Leg it?"

"You and your mate lie on your backs on a plank and use your feet to walk the boat along the walls. I can't do it – too small. Dad has to hire a legger when we get to the big tunnels."

Jane patted the horse on the neck. "What do you do with Nettlebed?"

"He goes up and over of course! We get to see some rare views."

By now they had left the city of Oxford behind and were out in the fields. Georgie pointed to a thicket over to their left. The reeds creaked and rustled in the breeze, pale stalks topped by flaglike seed heads.

"This was the first place I thought of when you said your dog had gone missing. That's where I would hide if I were the runaway. Too boggy underfoot to bring in horses, and the swamp won't hold much of a scent for the bloodhounds."

"How far does this stretch?" asked Jane. She could see no end to the nodding reeds.

"A long way, almost to the Thames that lies over yonder. The canal and river run side by side for a while, the river bending and meandering, the canal cut straight. This is soggy land round here, river meadows between the two. This time of year you have to wade, and I wouldn't like to say how deep the water gets."

Jane stopped talking to listen. The reeds hissed and hidden birds let out peeping cries. She opened her mouth to call Grandison, but Georgie stopped her with a firm shake of her head.

"Don't! We don't want everyone to know what we're about." She nodded to two soldiers who were riding down the path towards them, harness jingling. "Let's keep going and look for a break in the reeds. If a man went in that way, or a big dog, we should see some sign."

Jane closed her mouth and stepped behind Georgie so she didn't have to say anything to the soldiers. The men slowed their horses, and one thrust out a crude picture of Gardiner for Georgie to look at.

"Hey, you there! Have you seen this man?"

Georgie rubbed Nettlebed's nose as he scented the soldier's horses and tossed his head. "No, sir, can't say that I have."

"He is a dangerous man – broke out of prison. If you see him, get word to us and we'll deal with him. Don't try anything yourself."

"Wouldn't dream of it, sir."

The officer gave her a nod, cast a curious look at Jane, then decided to carry on to the boat owner and his guests to repeat his questions. His tone was more respectful when he realized Henry and Cassandra were listening.

"He's only saying that last bit because they want to claim the reward themselves," murmured Georgie.

The soldiers must have received a similar answer from Mr

Carter as Georgie gave them because they soon spurred their horses on to gallop to the next boat.

"Good. I'm glad they're gone," said Georgie.

"You are? Why?"

"Look." Georgie had slowed Nettlebed to a creeping walk. She pointed to a place in the reeds where the stalks were crushed and broken. Someone or something had recently gone that way.

Chapter 18

Jane was about to launch herself into the gap when Georgie caught her arm.

"Don't!"

"But Grandison!"

Georgie rolled her eyes. "Have you got no more sense than a minnow? You can't go blundering in like that!" Jane wanted to defend herself, but really she couldn't think of anything to say because Georgie was right. "Besides, I didn't say it was a path made by your dog and the prisoner. It could be made by a deer, or one of the mounted men searching for him. It's only the first clue."

Jane felt a little foolish. She knew from her own investigations that one little sign was only part of a puzzle, not the whole picture. "Then why bring us out this way? What can we do?" She wanted to throw back her head and howl her frustration.

Georgie clucked her tongue and started the horse walking again. "You need to be patient, Miss Jane. Learn from Nettlebed here. Those reeds over there – they stretch all the way up to the Duke's Cut." That was a vast area; Georgie was correct that Jane could do nothing running off into that labyrinth except lose her way. "The Cut was dug in the ground on the land beyond the reed beds. It curves to the Thames. That's where I'm taking you. Up there is a proper path heading into the reeds, an old one used for centuries by the people of Wolvercote." Georgie pointed out the roofs of the first houses of the village now becoming visible on the far bank. "The ground is firmer, and I think there's a cabin – a rotten old place – somewhere not too far in. Dad and I think that's the place to look – somewhere a local man might know. And Gardiner's a local man."

"The officers don't know about it too?"

Georgie grinned. "Doubt it. Most of them aren't from round here and it's not on any maps. It used to belong to a tinker, but he abandoned it when the duke began the works. Most people think it's sunk into ruin, but we heard about it from the navvies who fixed it up a little. They used it for shelter when they were digging out this part of the canal a year or so ago – a spot to eat their dinner out of the rain."

Jane was already repenting her rashness. Georgie clearly knew the area so much better than she did, and Jane was not making a good impression as a girl of sense. It was just that where Grandison was concerned, her usual level-headedness flew away. And she knew something that Georgie didn't: Gardiner had supplied the Canal Company, so he would've had plenty of opportunities to talk to the men working on it and could have found out such secrets as they knew.

They passed a village green and, beyond that, a pretty white inn with men enjoying their tankards of ale on benches outside. On the green, a flock of geese bustled forward in challenge and honked; women looked up from spreading out their sheets in the sunshine. Their expressions were not welcoming of the canal folk.

"Humph, their faces will turn the milk sour," muttered Georgie.

"They don't like you?"

"They accuse us of stealing their linen," said Georgie in a resigned tone. "Or sending our dogs to muddy the washing. They assume we're all troublemakers. That's why they have the geese to guard it. Geese make the best guard dogs."

Jane's own village of Steventon nurtured similar prejudices towards wandering bands of gypsies: two worlds that distrusted each other, the travellers and the settled folk. It was a melancholy thought to find this same attitude between canal and bank dwellers.

"Was the Duke's Cut really made by a duke?" Jane asked, determined to listen to Georgie this time.

"Aye. It's a grand scheme, built by the duke who lives in that big palace over there – Been-him or something like that." Georgie gestured towards what Jane took to be the famous estate of Blenheim, one of the most magnificent houses in all England.

"Blenheim. It belongs to the Duke of Marlborough."

"Sounds like the right man." Georgie did not sound overly impressed by titles. "Big dukes need big money for their big houses, so he dug a channel from the canal to the Thames and charges for us to use it."

They were approaching the Cut now – a little spur off the main channel with its own lock.

"It's a neat arrangement," continued Georgie. "His High and Mightiness can send supplies to his paper mill, which he built down there." She pointed, but if a factory lay that way, it was hidden in trees. A barge carrying bales of paper was currently waiting for the lock to fill, so Jane took that as evidence of the mill's existence. The thought of all that paper made her green with envy: with a few sheets from just one of those bales she could write stories to keep her family laughing all year.

"Lots of books come out of Oxford and you need something to print them on," Jane said, thinking what use would be made of so much paper.

Georgie shrugged. "Never had a book but I've seen them for sale. Fearful expensive they are."

Jane's estimation of the attraction of life on the canal plummeted. *No books?* "That's true."

"Especially the ones with pictures. I like those ones. Saw one once."

Jane agreed, though she liked the ones with stories the most.

The paper barge came out of the lock, making room for the *Mary-Ann*. Georgie and her father began their well-honed process of guiding the boat into the lock and closing the gates. The lock-keeper came out to take their toll. Henry dug into his pocket to pay, which was only fair as the Austens were the reason for this little expedition. Cassandra stepped ashore to join Jane on the bank.

"I saw you talking to Georgie and didn't want to interrupt. Does she have any idea where we should look? I was examining the bank for signs as we travelled but couldn't see any hint of Grandison."

Jane quickly brought her up to speed with the explanation about the boggy reed beds and the cabin.

Cassandra clasped her hands to her chest. "You mean she thinks Gardiner might be hiding out like Hereward the Wake?" The Austens all loved history, and the story of bold Hereward who hid from the Norman kings in the Fenlands was one of their favourites.

"Not like Hereward," said Jane. "He was a hero! But the rushy island does feel somewhat similar, I will allow."

Cassandra surveyed their surroundings. "Then what is our next move?"

"We should go and spy on the cabin – see if we can spot any sign of Grandison or the convict." Jane looked over at her brother. "Henry will insist that it is he who goes."

Cassandra sighed. "Yes, he will. He'll make us promise to stay by the barge. Will you keep your word?"

Jane was well aware that if she made a fuss about going herself, Henry would turn around and take them home. Her older brother had his moments of taking his responsibilities seriously – a possibility of encountering a dangerous fugitive was likely to be just such an occasion. And perhaps he was right: what could she do against such a one? Sense was winning the day. "I will."

Smiling in sympathy, Cassandra nodded. "Then let's tell him what Georgie told you and make a plan."

Jane sat on the bank, Rag-N'-Bone's head in her lap. The plan left her minding the barge while Cassandra and Georgie took Nettlebed a little way on to the horse trough to have a well-earned drink. Mr Carter and Henry had already left to follow the reed path to the cabin.

"Not a bad life for a dog," she told the Jack Russell. "I wager you like it."

The dog shifted so she could scratch his stomach. If Grandison were watching, jealousy would bring him out if nothing else did.

"I'm getting pins and needles. Let's stretch our legs." She'd spotted a glint of water through the trees. It looked like a little pond just behind the lock-keeper's cottage, in the opposite direction to the reeds so likely safe to explore. Parting the branches at the edge of the towpath, Jane discovered a circular pool with a heron wading at its edge.

"Would you look at that!" she exclaimed to the attentive Jack Russell. "Almost completely hidden and yet so close to the path." Remembering her promise not to leave the boat, she didn't go to the pond as she wanted but admired it from where she stood. Rag-N'-Bone had made no such promise though. A twig cracked. He shot off and bounded through the undergrowth like a dolphin leaping from the waves, barking in excitement. A second volley of barking joined in. She recognized that gruff tone.

"Grandison?" called Jane.

Then, to Jane's horror, a man lurched out from behind a holly bush, so close to her she could smell his sweat of fear. He stumbled towards her and gripped her arms, breath stinking of raw onions.

"Miss, I'm innocent I tell you!" he said fiercely. "You have to believe me!"

Jane opened her mouth to scream, but he quickly changed his grip to cover her lips and pulled her off the path.

"No, no, don't scream! I beg you!" He snatched a furtive glance around him.

Jane's breaths were coming in shallow pants. Grandison bounded up and growled, not liking what he saw.

"Quiet, dog: I mean your mistress no harm!"

Grandison was not convinced but he backed up, hackles raised. The Jack Russell had disappeared completely. Jane hoped he'd gone to fetch help.

"I saw you watching – and then your dog attached himself to me. It's a sign, I thought, a sign that God hasn't forgotten me. Your father's a clergyman, correct?"

Jane nodded jerkily, hating the taste of his dirty skin against her lips. He smelled of sweat and mud.

"Tell him Gardiner says he's innocent. He was set up by the Canal Company. They're the real villains. They want me silenced. Do you understand me?" Gardiner glanced over her head and must've seen something. "Your friends are coming back. Promise me you'll take the message?"

Jane certainly had no intention of hiding this encounter from her father. She nodded. Refusing did not bode good things for her.

"And give me a chance to get away now? The militia have orders to shoot on sight: I heard them say so."

Could she agree to that? Wasn't it her duty to report where she saw him?

"Please, Miss: you're my only chance to clear my name. I need time – and someone who will look into my story. I never cheated anyone, I swear it; I'm the one who's been cheated: cheated out of my shop, my good name, and my life."

Jane slowly nodded. She would tell her father but wouldn't speak before then. And if the militia were going to shoot before asking questions? She didn't want any man's death on her conscience.

The man inhaled, steeling himself for her reaction, and let her go. Jane steadied herself and turned to face him. Their eyes met for one brief moment, his full of pain and expectation of disappointment, hers…? Well, hers were probably full of doubt, she thought.

"Do what you must," he said. With a nod, he sank back behind the screen of the holly bush.

Jane straightened her clothing, wiped her wrist across her mouth, and took a steadying breath. Her body quivered, working through the shock and the excitement of the encounter. His manner was rude and rough, but she had sensed no falsehood in him. If he were guilty as charged, would he be staying near to Oxford? Wouldn't he have hurried away to lose himself in a place no one knew him, one of the big cities like London or Bristol? She would keep her word and tell her father. He would know what to do.

Grandison bounded over, bursting with joy to be reunited with his mistress. Jane hugged him, taking comfort in his familiar doggy smell.

"Yes, I love you too," she murmured. "But whatever are we going to do now?"

Chapter 19

Seated in Henry's rooms, teacup sagging in his hand so that it slopped onto the rug, Mr Austen was lost for words. He opened his mouth, closed it, opened it again, then shook his head at his daughter. Jane was crouched near the fireplace, arm around Grandison, glad that Henry had lit the fire. She was still shivering: shock and cold felt very similar, she thought, in an oddly dulled frame of mind.

Cassandra moved silently across the room and took the cup from his hand, placing it back on the tea tray.

"He said all this to you?" asked Mr Austen. "Gardiner?"

Jane nodded, hand on Grandison's collar. At the Duke's Cut, everyone had rejoiced that her dog had come back "of his own accord", as she put it; no one had suspected Jane had had an adventure of her own. Well, perhaps Cassandra had suspected something was up, but she had refrained from asking questions after one plea from Jane not to press her. This was a tale Jane wanted to tell once, and only with her papa present. Cassandra had bitten her lip and helped divert attention away from Jane as they said goodbye to their narrowboat hosts, abandoning the canal path to take a more direct route through market gardens and orchards that lay north of Oxford to their lodgings on St Giles. Mr Austen, summoned by Henry, had arrived only a few minutes later, just long enough for a kettle to boil, to rejoice at the return of the lost dog. Once all were gathered, Jane knew then that her reprieve was over. She'd embarked on the full tale when they were safely seated with tea in hand.

"Oh Jane." Mr Austen shook his head. He looked as shocked as she felt.

"Did I do the wrong thing?" Jane had really been trying her best, but she wondered if she had made a poor choice. "I did give my word."

"Only because the bounder threatened you!" growled Henry. "You should've told me. My little sister! He deserves horsewhipping, seizing you like that! I could've—"

"Could've what? Run after a desperate man who has already evaded all the search parties?" Her voice rose a notch. She'd managed to be calm, but her control was slipping now she was safe. Jane understood that her brother was offended she had not turned to him with her problem, but he wasn't her father. She trusted both Mr Austen's age and experience. Henry, as he had just demonstrated, would've been more likely to rush off to avenge what he saw as an insult, instead of giving it the consideration it needed. A man's life hung in the balance.

"You could've been hurt!" said Mr Austen, revealing that his shock was for the "might-have-beens" that were rushing through his mind. His baby girl had been in danger and he had not been there to keep her safe. She should've guessed that that would be the problem. She hadn't seen him this grim since she and Cassandra had narrowly survived a fever that had killed many of their friends. If she wasn't careful, Mr Austen was going to join her mother in putting her foot down and banning any trips outside Steventon. Jane loved her village, but she didn't want it to be the only place she saw all her life.

"But I wasn't in danger – not really. I believe that he had no intention of harming me." That was true, wasn't it? She'd been scared, and he'd been urgent with his demands, but he'd only held her firmly so he could speak without her screaming. "He was anxious to get the message to you and so was a little… rough in the manner of his delivery. That's not hard to understand. The militia aren't giving him much choice with their order to shoot him on sight."

"He's an escaped criminal," scoffed Henry.

"Who might be innocent." Jane rested her head on Grandison, preferring him to her brother just then. He didn't act as if her actions were foolish.

"There are no guilty men in prison if you believe their stories." Henry made himself sound worldly wise, so much more experienced than his naive sister who had swallowed the tale.

"Oh really?" asked Mr Austen, turning his attention on his son. "And you base that on what exactly?"

Henry flushed. "It stands to reason, Papa. Crimes are committed every day. Some people don't get away with it and are sentenced by the courts. They should take their punishment like a man and not complain they were caught."

"You don't know as much as you think you do, Henry." Mr Austen seemed almost disappointed in his son. "Have you ever been in a prison?"

Henry shook his head. "Thankfully no, I've not had that pleasure."

"Nor are you likely to. Have you asked yourself why so few people of our class are in there? Not because we are better than others, I can assure you of that. There is as much sin in the houses of the wealthy as the poor, maybe more as the temptation and scope to abuse power are so much the greater. But they also have the means to buy their way out of trouble, or are given lenient treatment by the men sitting in judgment because they see them as one of their own class." Mr Austen patted the footstool by his chair. "Come here, Jane."

Abandoning Grandison, who whined a little protest as he settled his head on his paws, Jane sat at her father's side and rested her head on his knee. His warm hand fell on her shoulder, rubbing soothing circles.

"No, you didn't do anything wrong. You gave your word. A promise like that is a sacred thing, and no one was injured by it. What remains for us to decide is what to do with the knowledge."

Jane mumbled something, a sound of agreement, but she was too exhausted by her adventure to lift her head.

"What are the choices, Papa?" asked Cassandra, stepping in when she saw Jane was too tired to carry on her part in the discussion.

"First, do we inform the authorities of Jane's encounter?"

Silence fell. Young ladies had to be very careful of their reputation, even ones as young as Jane. To have been in the company of a low fellow like Gardiner and not immediately raised the alarm would not be thought correct behaviour. Correct behaviour would have been to scream and swoon, if novels were anything to go by, thought Jane sourly. Or maybe she should have run round mad first, before swooning.

"Yes, I think we are all agreed that it is not wise to alert them now," continued Mr Austen. "Gardiner will probably have taken the precaution of moving his hiding place, so such a report would only cause us embarrassment and prove useless. We will tell no one – not even by letter, Jane."

Jane nodded.

"And you, Cassandra, no letters. I'll tell your mother when we get home."

Henry went over to a chest, rummaged inside, and next thing Jane knew he was draping a warm blanket over her shoulders. "Are you going home, Father?"

"Not immediately, no. That takes us to our second choice: either we ignore the man's plea or we look into it for him. If he is a victim of a miscarriage of justice, I would like to help him."

Of course he did. Her father was a saintly man.

"Sadly, innocent or not," continued Mr Austen, "he will still face the charge of absconding from prison."

"That's not fair," murmured Jane.

"I know, my dear, but it is the law." Mr Austen sighed. "But perhaps you girls should go home on the mail coach, changing at Newbury. You should be able to manage the journey together."

Jane sat up. "What? No!"

Mr Austen smiled. "I thought that might wake you up. Jane turn her back on a puzzle? Never! If you'd agreed I would have insisted on calling the doctor."

"You… you were joking?"

Her father tipped his head to one side as if listening to his own mind. "Not exactly, but I could have predicted your reaction. I take it you want to see this through? I have to warn you: the outcome might be very grim indeed. It might end on the scaffold."

Jane looked to Cassandra and then to Grandison. Both returned her gaze with dogged determination. "We're staying."

Mr Austen reached for his teacup and took a sip. "I just hope I don't regret it."

Chapter 20

"I can't believe you didn't tell me." Cassandra's voice was small in the dark of their attic room.

Grandison grumbled in his sleep but didn't wake. He lay on the rug between the two beds. If Jane reached across him she probably could touch her sister's hand, but she didn't feel like it just then. She had too many emotions crammed inside her, and she wasn't sure she could wedge her sister's hurt on top of it all. She'd be rattling along like an overloaded harvest cart, shedding barley stalks on the way to the barn.

"I did tell you," said Jane. "You were sitting right there."

"Only when you told everyone else."

Ah, that was what really upset Cassandra.

"I'd promised Gardiner," Jane said finally.

"But it's me. Your sister." Cassandra sat up and thumped her pillow into shape before flopping down again. "If I were in your shoes, I would not have held my tongue until we got back. I would've told you at the first opportunity."

Maybe, but if Jane had told her on the journey home, Cassandra might've been so outraged that she called in the nearest militia company to hunt him down. She tended to have her head turned by redcoats. They had passed several mounted officers on the way back. Jane had not wanted to risk it.

"Lives were at stake, Cassie, and giving my promise matters to me."

That argument did not go down well. "I thought we had an agreement that we tell each other everything – that I'm an exception to that kind of promise? Telling me is like telling yourself!"

Was it? Jane wondered. They were inseparable, but that wasn't the same as being one person, knowing all the other knew. Jane had a strong instinct for guarding her private thoughts, the place in her mind where she cultivated the source of her imagination; she had to hide that even from Cassandra. "What would you have done in my place?" she asked instead.

"I would've screamed and called for help." Cassandra sounded quite sure about it, proving that they were not at all the same person. "But you didn't do that, Jane, did you? You took a foolish risk with your safety."

Where was this coming from? Cassandra sounded much crosser than she should have been. Hadn't Jane been the victim in the encounter? It wasn't as if she'd thrown herself in the convict's path. She had restrained her impulse to rush into the reed beds after listening to Georgie; she hadn't insisted she go to the cabin with Henry and Mr Carter; she'd stayed quietly by the boat, as everyone had told her, and yet the adventure had still found her.

"That's not fair, Cassandra." Jane's sense of grievance swelled. Of course, she knew her sister was lashing out because she was hurt, but that wasn't an excuse.

"You always throw yourself into these things, trouble finding you even when we all think you're safe. I'm worried that one day you'll end up somewhere and you won't be able to get out of it."

Worry was a slightly better motive than jealousy, Jane would allow her sister that. "Ha-ha, I could say it is the pot calling the kettle black! Who was it who insisted on getting in George Watson's carriage and ended up flying out of it with a broken arm?"

"Humph!" When Cassandra was reduced to inarticulate grunts, Jane knew she had scored a point.

"That accident meant I was the one sent off to Southmoor Abbey, where I had to survive a fire in the library and the Abbey ghost!"

Silence was her only answer.

"In any case, Cassie, I think we should be worrying about poor Mr Gardiner rather than ourselves."

"*Poor* Mr Gardiner! You have changed your tune!"

Jane sighed and let her hand dangle on Grandison's gently rising ribcage. Little twitches told her he was in a doggy dream. It was comforting. "I've had a chance to think."

"You never stop. Your brain whirls like a grandfather clock, chiming out your great ideas at regular intervals." Cassandra thumped her pillow again. That sorry item was going to split its seams, feathers everywhere, if she were not more careful.

"True." Jane rather liked that image. She should make a note of it. "However, I've decided that I might have jumped to a conclusion that he was guilty based on what he looked like, all big and muddy, with a scowl that could strike you down at a hundred yards. In fact, I was plain scared of him."

"It's natural to be scared of men in prison uniforms."

"Yes, but if he is innocent – as he claims – then his appearance does him a disservice. The first impression he makes will persuade most people to look no further. Imagine him standing in the dock: a judge would glance up and think, 'there stands a man who must be guilty of something' and send him off to prison."

"But you've decided that you believe him – that he didn't cheat his customers?"

Jane stared up at the ceiling not many inches above her head. A faint light came in through the skylight. Somewhere the moon was gliding in and out of the silken clouds. Was Gardiner looking up at the same moon and pinning all his hope on a girl delivering his message for him? It was a very slender thread, like the finest cotton he once sold to the housewives and seamstresses.

"I was thinking that if he were guilty, and even if he were innocent, his best choice would be to get as far out of the area as he can. Once beyond the borders of Oxfordshire, he is unlikely to be followed, as his crime is not one to raise a public hue and cry. He's hardly a highwayman or a murderer. He could disappear, adopt a new name, join the army, go to America – he has so many more choices. And yet…"

"And yet he stayed here to clear his name. I see what you mean." Jane was pleased to hear the softening in her sister's tone. Cassandra was coming around to Jane's way of thinking. "But if that's the case, what can we do to help him?"

Jane turned on her side and smiled at her sister, who was facing her, dark eyes shining in the moonlight. "I'm so pleased you asked. Here's what I think we should do."

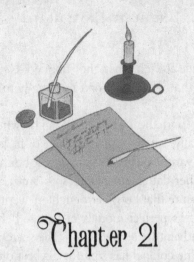

ᗡhapter 21

The next morning, they breakfasted in Henry's rooms. Mr Austen announced his intention to return to the prison to raise the case with his old friend, the Governor, hoping at the very least to see the trial records and discuss the possibility that there had been a miscarriage of justice. Henry, to his great regret, had to attend lectures, having missed quite a few, what with the rowing and his family's visit.

"I cannot risk being the family ignoramus, not with Jane and Papa about," he sighed dramatically.

Cassandra mock-boxed his ear for that comment.

"Will you girls be able to entertain yourselves?" asked their father.

That was better than Jane had hoped.

"No going out of the centre of the city." Mr Austen wagged his finger at them.

"Yes, Papa," they said meekly.

"No canal, or river – and definitely no rambling in the countryside to the north of here. You are not to venture anywhere near the place you saw the unfortunate."

With a glance at each other, they nodded. Neither had any desire to risk that when they had nothing helpful to tell the poor man.

"I had to report the sighting last night when you went to bed. Naturally, I kept your name out of it, Jane." Indeed, their mother would do more than mock-box an ear if she found one of her daughters' names so besmirched. Her life's goal was to ensure that both her daughters went down in the family records as perfect models of female behaviour, with not a hint of adventure about them. "The search is resuming at first light. The colonel has sent for his best bloodhound."

Jane rubbed her heart, feeling a twinge there. She sent a little prayer for Gardiner's safety while the Austens tried to work out the truth of his conviction. Little good would it do to prove his innocence only to find that he had been killed or seriously injured in the attempt to recapture him. She did not think he would come quietly if he had no cause to hope his appeal had been heard.

"Keep Grandison with you," concluded Mr Austen.

"Gladly," said Jane. "I fear if we let him off the leash, he will head back to his new friend."

Mr Austen gave a harrumph and ruffled the dog's ears. "Like him, do you? Well, you might be a better judge of character than many a human."

Grandison licked his master's hand in agreement.

With their menfolk thus disposed of, that left Jane and Cassandra to begin their investigation. After greeting Jenkinson and waving to Benjamin on his errands, they turned towards the city centre.

"I take it you are sticking to the plan?" said Cassandra.

Jane nodded. "So far we've only heard from those who have

decided they don't like him – those customers in Mr Lucas's shop and the assistant. The former didn't really know him so are swift to jump on the chance to tear someone to shreds with their gossip, and the latter actually said it came as a surprise. That suggests he previously held a good opinion of Mr Gardiner. We need to find someone who knows him much better than any of these."

"Jane, we were told that his family have gone back to his wife's home and aren't in Oxford. We promised Papa we'd stay in the city." Cassandra sounded genuinely worried that Jane would take it into her head to dive onto a coach to wherever the unfortunate Mrs Gardiner had retreated.

"I'm well aware of what we promised and I've made no such plan." She stopped and looked up at the heavens. "Lord, when did my sister come to think I was such a numbskull?"

Cassandra tugged her forward. "You're making a scene!"

"Oh Lord, enlighten her poor benighted mind as to the true brilliance of her sibling." Jane was enjoying herself now, embarrassing Cassandra in the middle of Oxford. What did it matter? No one knew them here.

"Jane!" whispered Cassandra.

"Let her foul nasturtiums be cast away from me." Jane howled it like a street preacher, causing Grandison to cock his head in interest. "Or is that 'aspersions'?" She grinned at Cassandra.

"I'm planting nasturtiums in your bed when we get home." Cassandra finally managed to get Jane walking again, blushing as the locals watched them and shook their heads.

They waited outside Lucas's shop until there was a lull in the customers.

"Let me handle this," said Cassandra, sailing into the shop just as their mother would do in her place. Jane tied Grandison to a post and followed.

"Back again, Miss?" said the assistant. He clearly had a good memory for attractive young lady customers. "I hope the lace was to your satisfaction?"

"Indeed, sir, it was perfect. I was wondering if I might look at your stock to see if there is anything else that takes my fancy." Cassandra smiled winningly, and Jane knew he would now do anything for her.

Jane wandered between the tightly packed shelves, breathing in the scent of rolled fabrics. Was that smell the dye used to make the colour, or was she smelling the sandalwood sprinkled to deter the moths? She fingered a woven cloth: flecked wool, the kind that country gentlemen favoured for their long winter coats. Henry would enjoy striding across a field in a garment made of this, shotgun slung over one shoulder while Grandison sniffed out the game birds. There were patterns for making the garment at home. Leafing through, she wondered for a moment if she would ever take on so difficult a task. Shirts and patchwork quilts were one thing, but a tailored jacket sounded above her skill at the moment.

And there was the little problem that she had no money to buy even half a yard of the fabric. That would make Grandison a jacket but not her brother.

"This would look very well on my sister's gown," said Cassandra, holding up an ugly length of cherry-coloured lace. Jane resisted rolling her eyes at Cassandra; they both knew that with her reddish complexion that was the last colour she should put near her cheeks.

"Indeed, the young lady has impeccable taste," enthused the assistant.

"I suppose your customers have been talking of the escape?" Cassandra said it in a tone that invited confidences.

"Indeed. We were all shocked to the bone. We truly did not know the man."

"Did you ever work for him?" Cassandra was now unwinding a pale lemon card of lace, holding it up to the light.

"Me? Heaven forbid!" The assistant was surprised into a rather rude rejection of the idea.

"You had more sense, I take it?"

"Indeed, I did. Not like Reuben." His eyes went to the stockroom at the back of the shop. "How he loved to crow over me when he was Gardiner's man; now he's our servant. And he was lucky to get that – tarred with the same brush, you understand me?" The assistant looked smug. "But Mr Lucas is a fine gentleman, quick to show compassion to the unfortunate, and Reuben does know his muslins, I have to grant him that. Send him to the warehouse rather than Mr Lucas or myself and we don't get swindled with the cheap stuff that way." He frowned. "Though I suppose it does take one to know one…" His voice trailed off as he lingered on this less than flattering thought about poor Reuben.

"This one please." Cassandra broke into his contemplation by choosing a length of lace. Jane couldn't see which from where she stood trying to peer into the stockroom. She caught a glimpse of a very pale youth, hair almost white, who was blacking boots by the meagre fire. She cast a glance over her shoulder to where money was being exchanged. Cassandra had better not be buying the cherry lace for her even as a joke.

Purchase made and a new customer arriving at that moment, the girls made their escape.

"Did you hear?" Cassandra asked as soon as they were safe from being overheard.

"You did very well – and I think I spotted Reuben too. Fair hair, lean, about twenty. He was doing chores in the back of the shop."

"What now?"

Jane cast about and saw a tea shop on the High Street with a view of the side door of the draper's down the alleyway.

"I suggest we retreat over there and keep watch. He will doubtless come out at some point on an errand or delivery. We'll take it in turns to keep an eye out for him. Do we have enough funds for tea?"

"And cake." Cassandra patted her purse. "Some of us don't spend all our money on paper and ink."

"Ah yes, but how would we write a letter home while we wait if I did not?"

Dear Frank,

Cassandra and I are aware how much you are consumed by a passion for following the latest fashions (or so we would wish, as what else have two sisters got to talk to their brother about?). You often tease us for our adoration of the latest designs that circulate in our little village, patterns that guide our needles and ensure we appear at our best on Sundays before the discerning eyes of our neighbours, so we thought we would send you what lessons à la mode we are learning during our time away from home.

As our esteemed elder brother Henry is now a fixture of the Oxford scene, we will enlighten you as to what the gentlemen of his acquaintance are wearing, selected from the fashion plates available at the best draper's the city has to offer.

Now our question to you is: which of the following is the garb of the guilty? We would warn you against the folly of trusting in appearances.

Yours affectionately,

Jane and Cassandra

Chapter 22

The Austen sisters were on their second pot of tea when Reuben finally emerged from the back door. As Jane had anticipated, he was loaded down with parcels – deliveries for local customers, she guessed. Cassandra settled their bill as Jane untied Grandison, who had been lying morosely outside, head on paws, unimpressed by the shop's "No dogs" policy. Jane had thought it prudent, as Grandison and cake was never a good combination.

"How shall we do this?" asked Cassandra as they set off in pursuit. Reuben held a list in his hand, which he was checking. That made their task easier as they could fall into step behind him without being noticed.

"As our father would say, honesty is the best policy." Jane sped up and tapped the young man on the shoulder. He looked up, startled.

"Did I drop something?" He glanced down at his parcels and then at her empty hands. There was something defenceless about him, like a baby bird, blind and featherless, just out of the egg.

"My apologies for interrupting you," said Jane quickly. "My sister and I have a few questions." Grandison woofed. "And my dog too, of course."

Reuben looked down at Jane's pet, and his face screwed up with suspicion. "I'm sorry but isn't that the dog that went missing? The one that followed my... the prisoner?"

Jane would pledge her next pin money that he had been about to say "my master". Did that hesitation mean that he was in contact with Gardiner still? "How do you know that?"

"I saw the posters. Black patch over one eye." True enough: they had made Grandison famous with their reward notices.

"Yes, this is he," said Cassandra. "He spent a day with Mr Gardiner and was returned unhurt."

Reuben nodded, relieved. "Good. Now if you don't mind?" He gestured to his parcels. "I'm a busy man."

"Let us walk with you and we'll ask our questions on the way," suggested Jane. Cassandra flanked him on the other side.

He shrugged, not looking at all pleased by the idea, but they had caught him between them. "It's the king's highway: I can't stop you following me."

They began walking again. Reuben made for the cobbled passage of Queen's Lane, uneasy with his escort.

"It's about Mr Gardiner," said Jane.

Confusion cleared, and he cast her such a look of dislike that Jane was taken aback. "I see." His tone was clipped.

A possibility came to Jane. "We're not looking for gossip, or for scandal. We want to help."

Cassandra nodded vigorously, going in front and walking backwards a few steps so he could see from her expression how serious they were. "Our father is approaching the prison Governor this morning on Mr Gardiner's behalf."

Reuben paused at the corner where the lane bent between high college walls. It was a lonely spot, a place to talk unobserved. He gave a pained sigh, obviously deciding he'd better get this over and done with. "Who are you again?"

Cassandra dipped a little curtsey. "I'm Miss Austen, and this is my sister, Miss Jane Austen."

"From Steventon in Hampshire," Jane supplied. "Our brother is a student here."

"I see." Though it sounded as if he really didn't.

Jane exchanged a quick look with her sister. She was going to have to displease her mother and confess what had happened the day before if they were to persuade him to talk. "When I was searching for Grandison, I met up with Mr Gardiner by mistake. We... er... stumbled across each other, you could say, in the fields to the north of Oxford."

Reuben's eyes widened. "You met Mr Gardiner? How is he? No, no, what I mean is, *why* is he still here? I thought he might have got away and I admit I rejoiced at the fact." He squeezed the parcels to his chest. Someone was going to take a delivery of very creased linen.

"He was..." Desperate? Wild? Distressed? "Eager to send a message that he is innocent."

"Of course he's not run. I knew it." Reuben sounded resigned. He let his parcels fall onto a mounting block and covered his face with his hands, scrubbing at his forehead as if to drive off the bad memories.

"You don't seem surprised?" probed Cassandra.

Jane thought she now knew who had left the file for

Gardiner under the bucket, but Reuben had been expecting the man to flee.

"No. I'm not," said Reuben. "He *is* innocent. I just thought he might've decided to stop struggling and make the best of his escape. But that's not Mr Gardiner's way. He'd prefer to die than let this slur remain on his good name."

This was very promising for their investigation: someone else who believed in his innocence. "Please, Mr Reuben, will you tell us what evidence you have that he isn't guilty as charged and why it wasn't brought up at the trial?" asked Jane.

The man gave a hollow laugh. "You are very young, Miss, and I suppose you've never been in a trial? Of course, you haven't. Nor had I until the last assizes. I was the one who bought the Canal Company's cloth from the warehouse, so I know exactly the quality we obtained: the very best. I know it was delivered to the headquarters because I oversaw that myself, straight into the housekeeper's closet." He kicked a stone in frustration. It pinged off the wall opposite. "Yet in a trial that lasted all of two hours, the Canal Company's housekeeper and Mr Herbert swore that the cheap stuff was what we had sent, and my witness to the contrary was dismissed as the misplaced loyalty of an employee."

"You kept on protesting?"

"Oh yes, and I nearly got sentenced myself for being part of the conspiracy to defraud. Fortunately, Mr Gardiner saw which way the wind was blowing and pleaded that any wrongdoing was entirely his responsibility. That tells you everything you need to know about the man." Reuben's eyes burned with angry pride. "He never forgets others even when he could've spun a story that I had been the one to make the exchange. I doubt that occurred to him, but even if it had he would never have stooped so low. His refusal to scapegoat me meant he carried the full weight of the supposed crime. They didn't even stop to ask if someone else might have done the deed."

Jane made a note that they now had a witness who could trace the good-quality linen from the warehouse to the customer. The exchange must then have happened in the company headquarters. "Do you remember the name of the housekeeper?"

"Oh yes. Mrs Younge. I believe she is the Secretary's widowed sister."

Jane had not liked Mr Herbert from the start and so had tried not to suspect him of anything nefarious, but this connection suggested he was in a prime position to enact the switch himself, or at least would want to protect one who did so if it had been his sister. That was helpful because they needed a suspect if they were to argue that Gardiner was not the right man in prison. Yet suspicions were going to be difficult to prove if all the evidence had been destroyed.

She looked up at the high walls around them, a seemingly insurmountable obstacle, much like the court verdict. Was there any hope? Greed might be the weakness. Was it likely that swindlers would want to destroy their chance of making a profit? If the original shipment was still in existence, too valuable to be got rid of…?

"Is there any way to identify the original linen you supplied?" she asked.

Reuben gave her an astute look. "You were not joking when you said that you are trying to help, were you?" He laughed again, a slightly less desperate sound. "Two young girls barely out of the schoolroom." Strictly speaking, Jane wasn't yet out, but she let that stand. "Is that what we've come to?"

Jane knew a rhetorical question when she heard one. She had to get him back to the task at hand. "But is there?"

Reuben picked up his parcels. "Yes. We ordered the damask to be figured with a bespoke pattern of roses and castles, a white satin on white pattern like a watermark, not obvious to the eye. Many of the narrowboats use them as decorations, and it was meant to be a nod to the Canal Company's business. Mr Gardiner always liked to go the extra mile for his customers, and it was to be a surprise when they spread the tablecloth for the meeting of the board – our thank you for such a valuable commission." He pulled a bitter face. "And look at all the thanks we got in return."

"Then they may never have known it was there if they didn't stop to untie the bolt of material?"

Reuben gave a grim smile. "And who is 'they' in that scenario?"

"The real thieves, of course!"

"Then no, they might not have seen anything if they sold it on as quickly as possible. Finest damask table linen, that's how it was described on the inventory."

They walked out of the narrow lane. Before them lay the sandstone ramparts of the Bodleian Library and the drum-shaped Sheldonian Theatre. Students and professors in black cloaks swooped by. Reuben's shoulders slumped as his brief moment of hope in the lane dissipated in the open spaces of the centre of the university.

"I wish I could produce a magic wand and make all this go away," he said, more to himself than to them.

"You must have suffered terribly." Cassandra was always good with comforting words.

"Me?" He seemed shocked that anyone could consider his feelings. "Yes. But that is nothing to Mr Gardiner's plight. His own family has been chased out of Oxford, his boys taught to curse his name for the disgrace he had brought upon them. I'll do anything I can to help him. If what I've told you will assist your father in clearing his name, then I will be eternally grateful to you both." An unseen clock struck the hour. "I had better run. I've some doctoral gowns to deliver to Wadham. If I'm late, I might lose the only job standing between me and ruin." He dipped his head and jogged towards the entrance to the college.

"Well," said Cassandra.

"Well," agreed Jane.

"What now?"

"Now? I think we need to rummage in some linen cupboards."

Sneaking into the Canal Company was going to be hard, if not impossible, as they had no business being there, so Cassandra suggested that a frontal attack might work as well.

"I'll distract them while you search," she said as they approached the building. "I'll ask to see Mr Herbert or to leave a message for him, something that Mrs Hill might want us to tell him. I'll come over a little faint and you can go in search of refreshment."

Jane agreed that this was the best course. People were quick to believe that delicate young ladies were fragile creatures subject to fits of weakness. Wandering the corridors in search of a glass of water from the kitchen would not be punishable, just annoying. Being found with no explanation would cause much more of a headache. "And if he's there?"

"Oh, I'll make up some nonsense about wanting my empty head filled." The sisters grinned at each other.

"Ask him to show you again where Liverpool is." They arrived outside, and Jane tied Grandison to the railing.

"Quite. While I do that, go for the housekeeper's room. If they kept the linen, it should be there."

They gazed up at the carved mermaid. Even Grandison cocked his head in interest. She seemed a very jolly personage to swim on the frontage of a building that had been the undoing of at least two men.

"I'm not sure they will have done that," Jane admitted, "but we have to look."

"Oh?" Cassandra patted Grandison's head in apology for leaving him behind for this adventure.

"Think about it. If Mr Herbert, or Mrs Younge, were behind the swap, they probably weren't expecting it to come to light. They would've paid for Gardiner's goods out of company money, exchanged them for poor stuff, and sold on the best quality to line their own pockets. When someone raised the alarm, they would've done everything they could to hide their trail."

"Yes, I see now."

"And my next guess is that this wouldn't have been the only time they did such a thing. Imagine the panic when their little game was spotted. They had to find someone to blame, and Gardiner was the easiest target – a local trader who struck people at first sight as dangerous, even villainous, because he has the misfortune to be built like a haystack."

"Then there's little point risking this?" Cassandra frowned at the mermaid.

"I'm hoping that there may be traces of their scheme, maybe records of the sale. I'll check the housekeeper's account books if they aren't locked away."

"Good plan." Cassandra took a bolstering breath. "Let us go in."

Chapter 23

Mr Herbert wasn't in the office, according to the footman who answered their knock. He was out checking the work of the remaining convicts, so Jane and Cassandra were able to implement their first plan of Cassandra asking to leave a note and Jane going in search of a glass of water for her wilting sister. Walking as quietly as she could down the flagged corridor, she reasoned that the kitchen and the housekeeper's room were likely to be in the less visible parts of the building, possibly in the basement, if there was one. Finding a servants' stair at the rear of the building, she followed it downwards and was rewarded with an area with many more people bustling about, all of them of the servant class. A maid was mopping the floor, removing evidence of a recent visit by the coalman, the air smelling of wet stone and soot. Jane could hear the clatter of crockery to her left, marking the most likely location of the scullery where the washing up from breakfast was underway.

Jingling keys behind her warned her of the approach of someone on the stairs. Indecision froze her to the spot for a second. Should she stay where she was with all her excuses ready or duck out of sight?

Instinct made the decision for her, and she dived into the nearest doorway, stumbled over a pile of what felt like rocks, and landed on her hands and knees. It was dark, and very, very dusty. There was an unmistakable odour in the air of coal. She stifled a groan: her dress and stockings, not to mention her hands, were going to suffer from this.

Coal rattled down the pile in a little landslide. Jane quietly picked herself up, but dislodged one lump. It carried on going and out of the door. Jane scurried back behind it.

"I see the coalman has delivered." The woman who spoke kicked the coal back into the storeroom.

"Yes, Mrs Younge," said the maid. "Mucky stuff."

It was the housekeeper! That might be a bit of luck if Jane could see which way the woman went. Jane put her eye to the crack in the door at the hinge.

"Indeed. Make sure you get it all up. I don't want any of that walked into the carpets upstairs. They're calling for claret in the boardroom. I'll just fetch the decanter. When you've finished here, come to the pantry and take it upstairs. Fresh apron, don't forget!" She disappeared into a room just down the corridor, emerged a moment later with a cut-glass decanter on a silver tray, and headed deeper into the building, presumably making for the wine cellar.

The maid gave a last swish of her mop, sighed, then wiped her hand across her brow. Rubbing the small of her back, she picked up the bucket and took it into the scullery to empty.

This was Jane's chance!

Jane crept out of the coal cellar and hurried to the housekeeper's room. Mrs Younge had not used a key to enter, but Jane was still relieved to find the door opened to her touch. She ducked inside – and just in time. In the corridor she heard the maid exclaiming over the new marks on her clean floor.

"I'll wring their neck when I find out who did this," she muttered, going back to the scullery to fetch her mop.

Jane glanced down at herself. She looked a fright, knees black, hands the same, skirt streaked with coal, as if she'd fought a chimney sweep and lost. There was a basin and towel on the housekeeper's washstand. Dare she? As she suspected the woman to have been party to sending an innocent man to prison, she did not worry too much about dirtying the water and towel. However, she would prefer for her presence here to go unnoticed until she was clear of the building. She tipped the water into a pot plant, wiped the basin, and tucked the blackened linen under the armchair by the fire.

Cleaning up had given her a chance to consider the room in greater detail. There was a desk and upright chair under the window. The glass did not give out onto the outside, but into the corridor so was poorly lit. In the dim light, she could see there were shelves of quality glassware. Silver was in a cupboard with a wire mesh frontage. That probably required one of the keys that the lady carried. One wall was taken up with linen cupboards. Jane opened the nearest and gaped at the huge amount stacked there: tea towels, hand towels, napkins, tablecloths, tray covers, lace doilies. It would be impossible to look all the way through; she would not be done before the lady returned to her room. But maybe it was instructive enough to see it all here? They had bought far more than a place of business could possibly need, and none of it was on show as far as Jane could remember from her own visit. There was enough here to start their own draper's shop.

"I wonder how much of this is destined to be sold on quietly," murmured Jane, touching the nearest doilies then pulling her hand back when she saw that her handwashing had been an inadequate process. A black smudge now graced the edge of the lace.

Deciding to implement her second plan – finding the books – Jane went to the desk. There was a household accounts ledger on the surface open at today's date. Had she ever known the exact date of Gardiner's supposed crime? No, she thought, but he had been convicted in the last assizes which had been in spring, so that put the deed he was accused of in the months before.

Glancing over her shoulder, fearing at any moment to hear the jingle of the lady returning, Jane flipped back the pages. Everything was meticulously listed, incomings and outgoings. A bookmark stood out on one page. Following a hunch, Jane turned to it and found the page that listed the delivery from Mr Gardiner's shop, a pencil mark in the margin showing how this had been reviewed and noted. Of course, this would have been evidence produced at the trial! That made it very unlikely the fate of the damask would be registered in the same place. It would be an incompetent swindler who noted down her own crime in the very same book as she shared with the authorities. This was a dead end.

Jane sighed. Sometimes she got carried away with a belief in her own cleverness. This whole expedition had been a waste of time, not to mention very risky. A sensible person would say she should cut her losses and retreat.

But then she looked around the room again. She might have misjudged the ease with which evidence would present itself, but she rarely misjudged human character. From her observations, people had a base of behaviour from which it was hard for them to deviate. The housekeeper's office was so tidy, the accounts so neat, surely someone with a mind like that wouldn't miss an opportunity to take note of what she had done with the bolt of material?

Jane decided to give herself another minute. If she turned nothing up in that time, then she would leave.

Kneeling, she began searching the desk, opening the drawers and feeling along the sides. She looked for hidden compartments or notes disguised as laundry lists. Nothing. The desk was as it seemed: a simple workaday table with plain drawers suited to a housekeeper. It had none of the expensive security measures, such as false bottoms or secret cubbyholes, that a gentleman's desk might boast.

Jane sat back on her heels, almost ready to admit defeat, when her eye alighted upon a sewing basket kicked to the back under the desk. Going down on all fours, she crawled to retrieve it.

A jingle came from the corridor. Jane had a split second to decide what to do. Escape was impossible. Dragging in her trailing skirts, she folded herself up into a ball and hid in the shadows under the table.

Mrs Younge came in accompanied by a man.

"You say the young lady wanted to leave a message?"

"Yes, ma'am. But she's waiting for her sister and won't leave without her." The man sounded like the servant who had answered the door to the Austen sisters. Jane realized that she had been gone a very long time; no wonder they had come looking. Cassandra must be tearing her hair out by now.

"Then there were two young ladies?"

"Indeed, ma'am. They came here before with Mr Herbert and their father, a clerical gentleman. They are lodging with Mrs Hill."

"Well, James, we can't have little girls running around the place. This is the headquarters of the Canal Company, not a nursery school."

Jane wrinkled her nose up at that. Nursery school indeed!

"One would think their mother would at least send them out with a governess, especially if the elder is prone to fainting fits. These well-bred girls should do a hard day's work and see how faint that makes them feel!" There was bitterness in her tone. Mrs Younge clearly resented her position in life.

"The younger one must've got lost looking for some water for her sister. We had better look for her or Mr Herbert might be cross with us."

"My brother wouldn't dare be cross with me!"

"Not you maybe, ma'am, but me – I don't have that defence."

"Oh, very well. I'll look around the ground floor, you search down here."

The two went out, keys jingling with every step. Jane thought of the "belling the cat" story her father often told them – her own experience of prior warning showed that it would've been very useful to the mice if they had found the courage to carry out the attempt.

Was there time for a last-minute rummage?

Dragging out the basket as she emerged from her hiding place, Jane felt inside among the balls of wool. At the bottom was a notebook. She had suspected something might be hidden there, because putting a workbasket under the desk was an inconvenience, not at all in keeping with the arrangements of a neat woman. Heart thumping, she flipped it open. There it was: a second list of accounts all laid out, neat as a pin. From a glance, Jane saw that it was not only household linen that had been sold on, but wine and coal, candles, and even beeswax polish.

How tempting it was to slip it into her pocket and make a run for it! But if she did that, all she would be left with was evidence of her own theft and no way of proving it belonged to Mrs Younge. The lady could deny ever having seen it. It had to be found in place if it were found at all. Jane stuffed it back into the basket, kicked it under the desk, and hurried to the door.

No sooner had she stepped into the corridor than she heard a voice behind her.

"Oi! What are you doing here?" The footman hurried towards her, mouth pinched with irritation.

Jane decided it was time to act as Fordyce recommended in his sermons. She held up empty hands to show she hadn't taken anything. "I really don't know, sir," she said faintly. "I've gotten myself all turned around. I was looking for the kitchen but found a coal cellar, a linen cupboard, and not much else."

"You foolish girl! You are only a step or two from the kitchen! You should've asked a maid, not gone looking for yourself! This place is a warren down here."

"Indeed, it is. I became quite muddled. Would you be so kind as to take me back to my sister? I'm feeling quite overset." She gave a little sniff as if close to tears.

That scared the man into action. The last thing he wanted was to be in charge of a weeping female. "Yes, of course. She's just upstairs. What with her swooning and you crying, I really think you shouldn't venture into a place like this again. It's too much for refined young ladies." He took her gently by the arm and towed her up the stairs. "It's all right, Mrs Younge, I found the girl. She'd taken a wrong turn by the coal cellar!"

Mrs Younge met them at the top of the stairs, a worried Cassandra at her side. Her poor older sister must've been racking her brains to think up yet more excuses for their presence, as Jane was taking so long.

"There you are, Jane!" exclaimed Cassandra. "I was about to send out a search party for you!"

"This kind man already did," said Jane, looking sweetly up at the footman. "Thank you so much."

Politeness had the effect of disarming further reproofs. "Well then, you'd better get home. No more wandering off," said the footman gruffly.

Mrs Younge just scowled at them both. "Haven't you forgotten something?"

The girls looked at each other in alarm. Did she know?

"The message for Mr Herbert?" Mrs Younge said.

"Oh yes." Cassandra drew out a note and handed it over. "Come along, Jane." She seized her sister's arm and pulled her out of the building as fast as she could go without it being a run. Only once outside did she take a full breath, patting her chest as Jane untied Grandison. "Never again," she said in an undertone.

"Yes, that was a bit close, but let's get further away before we talk about it." Jane glanced over her shoulder and was not surprised to see Mrs Younge peering at them out of a window. She waved and gave a big smile, making the woman retreat quickly. "I don't think I like her." Her tone belied her enthusiastic gestures.

"Nor do I." Cassandra gave a more subdued wave, then turned away.

"What excuse did you leave in the note?"

"Just some nonsense about being on time for dinner."

They threaded through the crowds, making for their lodgings.

"And we've got good reason for our prejudice against Mrs Younge," said Jane, going on to explain her adventures in the basement.

Cassandra was suitably shocked at the full depths of criminality that Jane had uncovered. The worst was that the woman was happy to let someone else serve the prison sentence she deserved. "You left the notebook? What if she destroys it?"

"Why would she, unless she suspects I found it, and I tried not to leave any trace."

Cassandra wrinkled her nose. "Jane, have you looked at yourself recently?"

"No, why?"

"You're a walking coal dust cloud – the back of your skirt is a fright. If she keeps her room as neat as you said, she will know where you've been."

"Oh." Jane could have kicked herself for not thinking of that. "Oh dear. What do you think we should do? Tell Papa that we've been spying on the enemy?" They both grimaced at that thought. "I don't suppose we can make it sound like we did it by accident?" No, their father was too astute to buy that story. "We didn't think this through, did we? Either we get in trouble for our trespass, or she has time to get rid of a key piece of evidence that would help exonerate Gardiner."

Put like that, there wasn't much of a choice.

"Run?" said Cassandra.

And they did.

Chapter 24

They found their father praying in the chapel at St John's College. It was, of course, not unusual for a clergyman to be discovered on his knees at the altar rail, but under normal circumstances their father waited for a service to make his requests to the Almighty in a public place. Leaving Grandison outside with an obliging student, they crept in and knelt at the altar beside him, one on either side, not daring to break in on his conversation with his Creator. Their family was well trained by him, encouraged to bring their own prayers to God in times of need.

Having sent up her own petition, Jane had a moment to catch her breath. The chessboard tiled floor, white walls framing stained glass, and heavy oak roof beams were like a grand cousin to their own little church in Steventon, familiar yet daunting, someone with whom you had to be on your best behaviour. Jane peeked up at the altar, then raised her eyes to the image of Jesus and his angels in the window, sunshine glowing in the muted colours of white, blue, and gold. The sight settled her anxious thoughts. She believed with all her soul that her father would see that what they had done, they had done for the very best reasons, even if he disapproved of their methods. Mr Austen's faith meant he had unshakeable views when it came to love for one's neighbour: that was the greatest commandment. Gardiner, the disgraced and ill-treated prisoner, was their neighbour.

Mr Austen lowered his hands and got up from his knees to sit on the nearest pew.

"My dears," he said in a lowered voice, "why have you followed me in here?"

"Are you well, Papa?" Cassandra asked, likely sensing as Jane did a peculiar sadness about their father.

He gave her a faint smile. "Well in my person, but not in my spirit."

"Oh Papa!" Jane rested a hand on his arm. "Is there bad news?"

He nodded. "I talked to Governor Harris and saw the reports of the trial. From what I read, it was not fairly conducted. That sometimes happens when minds are made up and prejudice against an accused rules the day."

There was hope in that though, thought Jane, because it meant Mr Austen would be pleased to hear of more evidence coming to light.

"The alarm about the poor-quality linen was only raised when one of the board members complained. The housekeeper claimed not to have noticed, it being a new consignment, and said she was astonished now it had been brought to her notice. I do not find that a convincing excuse. Her protestations of innocence began the chain of accusations ending up with Gardiner in prison. I brought these inconsistencies to the attention of the Governor, and he said that, unfortunately, so many local gentlemen, including judges, have invested in the canal scheme that none of them would appreciate us casting any doubt on the operations of the same."

Jane's glimmer of optimism flickered out.

"But what about the truth... what about what is right?" asked Jane.

"Exactly my words to him, but he is a pragmatic man. His view is that, unless we can prove Gardiner's innocence beyond any shadow of a doubt, we have no chance of getting his case reopened." Mr Austen reached a finger under the edge of his wig and scratched above his ear, sending it a little askew in that adorable way of his. "And I'm afraid, even if judged innocent, Gardiner would still be guilty of escaping from prison. That is a crime, even if the man is not guilty of his original offence."

"But that's absurd!" Jane's voice was too loud, echoing around the solemn chapel. "Sorry." She forced her tone down to a whisper. "So he's to be damned if he does and damned if he doesn't?"

"Not in the eternal sense of the word," said her father. "We can trust God to be wiser than human judges, but in essence you are correct. The poor man is in an intolerable situation. That is why I am praying for him."

Jane looked back to the comforting smile of their saviour and his angels and took courage. They would expect her to tell the truth even if it cost her. "Papa, Cassandra and I have had a little adventure." She unfolded all that had happened since they went out that morning. Mr Austen's expression grew grimmer and fiercer as she spoke, hopefully not aimed at their antics but at the horrible behaviour they had uncovered.

An uneasy silence fell when she finished with the story of how they had left matters but that she might have left traces of her presence behind.

"I saw this Reuben's account in the trial, but it was dismissed as being merely to defend his master. You think he was telling the truth?" Mr Austen said at last.

"I do," said Jane.

"Cassandra?"

"I'm convinced of it, Papa."

He nodded, accepting their word. "And the notebook? You chose to leave it there?"

"I didn't take it because I thought that would mean Mrs Younge could deny it existed. I thought they might even claim I meddled with it."

He hummed as he considered her answer. "But if they know you've been in her room, they might say you planted it there to exonerate Mr Gardiner, though what possible motive a girl from quite another part of the world might have to do that, I don't know."

"But it would be the word of respected grown-ups against me," said Jane, seeing his point.

"Indeed – and the scandal would infuriate your mother."

The prospect of that floated before all three of them in the cool air of the chapel, their mother a St Michael with a sword ready to slay dragons.

"Then we can do nothing?" asked Cassandra.

"I did not say that," said Mr Austen. "But we need a plan – and a magistrate who is on our side, preferably one that has not invested in the canal scheme, if such a man is to be found in Oxford."

"What about Mr Lambton?" suggested Cassandra. "He is

a magistrate and lives in Berkshire – that is only one county over."

Mr Austen's expression lightened. "Closer than that; it lies on the western bank of the Thames. Half of the people of Oxford live there. In fact, Gardiner might very well be hiding out in his county. That's a very good thought, Cassandra. Mr Lambton would be respected by other magistrates if he could vouch for what you have discovered." Mr Austen rested his hands on his silver-topped cane and rubbed his thumb against the well-worn nub. "Henry." He tapped his cane.

"What about Henry?" asked Jane.

"We send Henry and Mr Lambton to the Canal Office. No doubt other young men could be persuaded to accompany them should any there seek to stand in their way. I will go back to the prison and persuade the Governor to come with me." Mr Austen rubbed his chin. "An anonymous informant should do the trick. It is imperative your names are kept out of it."

"You would lie to protect us?" asked Jane in a hushed voice.

"I'm not lying. I know your identity, but Governor Harris will not – meaning you will be anonymous to him." That was splitting hairs, but it did allow Mr Austen to keep his rule of never lying.

Maybe this would work? Jane imagined the scene: the men walking boldly into the Canal Company office and demanding to see the housekeeper's workbag. How easily they could be refused!

"Papa, I doubt they will let even a magistrate conduct a search on what will seem a whim or mischievous word of an anonymous person. They will probably demand a court warrant, and we don't have time for that." An idea came to her,

her memory returning to her first visit to the office. "I think we need someone who has a right to search the place."

Her father looked at her with interest. "I can see the wheels of your mind turning, Jane. Tell us what you are thinking."

"I know I'm but an empty-headed female with a mind of fluff and bonnets…"

Mr Austen chuckled.

"… But my understanding of the Canal Company is that it has shareholders, people who put in money?"

"That's right, as an investment."

"Then these investors own the company, in a sense?"

He nodded.

"If we could get one of them to search, even Mr Herbert could not refuse to let them into their house."

"A shareholder outweighing the Secretary. Agreed. But unfortunately, Jane, the hearts of men tend to reside in their pocketbooks. I doubt any of them will wish to damage a company that promises to repay their investment many times over, not over so small a thing as the fate of a tradesman from Oxford."

"Ah, but what about a son of a major investor, one who even has shares in his name, someone who is already on our side?"

A smile broke out across Mr Austen's face. "You mean Jenkinson?"

Jane nudged her sister playfully. "Cassandra, I think you should be the one to tell Mr Jenkinson that he has a chance to be a hero."

Jenkinson sat on a low stool by the hearth in the rooms he shared with Henry, a faint greenish tint to his already pale skin. His slender arms and legs were all akimbo, making him seem like a grounded daddy-long-legs.

"Miss Austen, you want me to march in there and demand to see the books?"

"Yes," said Henry bracingly.

"We know you can do it," said Cassandra with a winning smile.

Jane kept quiet and hugged Grandison.

"You cannot ask quietly; you'll have to be bold, act as if you own the place, channel your king of the coal industry manner!" elaborated Henry.

"I don't have a manner like that." Jenkinson gave them all a woeful look.

Henry slapped him on the chest. "You do, deep down."

Very deep down, thought Jane. It was a shame Jenkinson had not had the Austen upbringing of family theatricals, else this would be child's play for him.

"You are Henry V at the Battle of Agincourt," suggested Cassandra.

"Actually, Miss Austen, I always thought I was temperamentally more of a Hamlet," Jenkinson said sheepishly.

"But even he screws his courage to the sticking place at the end and fights," said Jane.

"And dies horribly." Jenkinson pulled a face.

"Nobly," corrected Henry.

"Perhaps think of yourself as Julius Caesar crossing the Rubicon to take Rome?" said Jane, remembering his fondness for classical examples. "Before the knife in the back, naturally." Maybe that hadn't been such a good image to conjure?

"You'll do it?" asked Cassandra, taking a more straightforward approach.

Jenkinson puffed out his cheeks and gave a jerky nod.

Henry hauled him up by his elbow. "Come on then, man, let's strike while the iron is hot. Lambton is bringing his father. We are to meet them in the lodge in five minutes. My father is bringing the prison Governor."

The two young men vanished down the stairs, leaving Jane, Cassandra, and Grandison alone. The old wood settled and creaked as if the room wanted to make its feeling known. Jane hoped it was approval. Cassandra put a little packet of lace in Jane's lap.

"For you."

It was the lemon lace, not the cherry. "Thank you, dearest."

"You deserve it."

They waited a few minutes in silence, but it was unbearable.

"I don't think I can just sit here," said Jane, "not knowing what happens. I've got to do something or run mad."

Grandison went to the door, nose pointing to the handle.

"I think Grandison is suggesting that we entertain him while we wait. Let's take him for a little walk." Cassandra got up and tied the strings of her bonnet.

"We should visit Georgie and Mr Carter. I'd like to know what news they have of the search." Jane clipped a leash on her dog.

"Oh, but won't Papa be cross we went back to the canal?"

"Not if we stay in town where they are moored. Gardiner and the search must be miles away by now." Jane opened the door to the dark staircase. "Besides, I feel they should know what happened yesterday at the Duke's Cut and all we've learned since."

It felt like a week had passed, not a single day, since Jane was confronted by Gardiner at the pond.

Cassandra made no protest, so they headed for the nearest way down to the canal, Grandison pulling at the leash as he sensed where they were going.

Georgie was polishing the brass on the horse's bridle when they arrived. She was back in her breeches, and Jane's opinion was that they looked much more natural on her than the dress she'd worn for guests. Mr Carter gave them a brief "how-do" before returning to his task of touching up the paintwork of castles and roses.

"You again," Georgie said with a grin.

"Yes, us. You can't keep your deckhands away now you've given us a taste of the life." Jane let Grandison off the leash so he and Rag-N'-Bone could make their greetings. They had progressed to sniffing friends as opposed to territorial rivals.

"I'm glad you came by. We're heading north tomorrow. Been here longer than we normally would."

"Then we are glad we came too," said Cassandra.

"Offer your friends some tea, love," called Mr Carter.

"That means he fancies a cup himself," said Georgie.

Mr Carter chuckled.

Georgie set the bridle aside and invited them to follow her into the cabin. Jane at last got her wish of seeing inside the narrowboat, the neat bunks, little stove, and cannily placed closets. There was a doll's house feel to the place that was quite enchanting. She opened a cupboard.

"Inspecting the shelves?" Georgie filled the kettle from the jug standing in a basin.

"Shelves in a closet: happy thought indeed," said Jane, shutting it again with a rueful smile. "Sorry. I'm inquisitive."

"She means nosey," said Cassandra.

They took the tea outside, Georgie handing a cup to her father.

"We have something to tell you," said Jane, "about the fugitive."

Over steaming cups, she and Cassandra explained the events following the trip to the Duke's Cut.

"Fancy not saying a thing to us! You have some steel in you, Miss Jane." Georgie's tone was approving. "The man's innocent, you say?" Georgie warmed her work-roughened fingers on her cup. "We'll pass the word. If he escapes and comes to one of us for help, he'll not be turned away."

Jane hadn't thought of that, but it was a good idea. "Thank you. It would be best perhaps if he could just slip away. The chance of proving him not guilty might have already gone by as he staged an escape, breaking another law."

Just as the Austen sisters were about to take their leave, there were shouts and cries from further up the towpath.

"Hold on," said Georgie, "you must get Grandison out of the way. It sounds like the militia are coming back."

Jane dragged a reluctant dog onto the little deck. Georgie moved Nettlebed so he was as far off the path as possible on the narrow way, though it was still a squeeze. Redcoats came into sight, riding two-by-two. They bounced along swiftly, bridles jingling, hooves pounding. The expression on the lead riders was jubilant. Jane's heart sank.

"Huzzah!" shouted one of the householders on the far bank. He waved his hat. "Huzzah!"

The militia trotted on, the front file passing the Carters'

boat. Then, in the midst of the riders, Jane saw a man being forced to run along, hands tied in front and attached to the saddle of one soldier. It was Gardiner. Their eyes met for the briefest of moments. Jane wanted to shout that she hadn't betrayed him, that in fact she'd done her utmost to clear his name, but he turned away. Whether his expression had been one of bitter disappointment, or an attempt to protect her by pretending not to recognize her, Jane could not tell.

The militia rode on. Gardiner would be back in prison within the hour.

The Austen sisters were silent. Georgie broke the quiet with a sigh. "I guess that is it then for him? No getting out again."

Her father cleared his throat. "He'll likely be sent to the Hulks in London, awaiting transportation, if they don't decide to execute him. It's a hard fate either way."

"Would they? Execute him, I mean?" asked Jane.

"Maybe, maybe not." Mr Carter scratched his chin. "There's one rule for the rich and another for the poor in this country. He was a man of means once-upon-a-time, so he might get treated with more respect than if a poor man was caught doing what he's done."

"But he's innocent!" Jane protested.

Mr Carter plucked the paintbrush from behind his ear to return to his task. "Not according to the law, and that's the verdict that matters in his case."

Georgie looked between the girls and her father. "Dad, could we stay on an extra day, to see what happens?"

Her father raised his brows. "We've a load to fetch from Coventry. And he's nothing to do with us."

"But he is misjudged by most. I think that makes him very like us."

Mr Carter looked at his daughter for a long moment. "All right. I can spare a day, though I think it will bring nothing but heartache. But then we must leave."

"I think his fate will be known very soon," said Jane, thinking of the men going to the Canal Company in search of evidence. "It would be good to know he has friends around, whichever way his story goes."

Jane feared, however, that this was one tale that would not have a just outcome.

And she did so want a happy ending.

Chapter 25

Jane and Cassandra arrived back at Mrs Hill's boarding house to find the dining room crammed with people. Mrs Hill had been ousted to take refuge in the kitchen with the maid, while the Governor of the prison, Mr Lambton, and Mr Austen confronted Mr Herbert with the evidence they had found. Henry had brought Jenkinson and what looked like his entire boat crew to witness the proceedings.

"Bad doings," said Mrs Hill in a not-so-quiet voice as the men rumbled away in her best room. She handed Jane a towel for Grandison's paws.

"Oh?" said Cassandra lightly, unbuttoning her coat. "What's going on?"

"It seems that Mr Herbert's own sister has been cheating him. Can you believe it? Poor man is shocked, so very shocked."

Jane could believe the first but doubted the second. "How do you know this?"

Mrs Hill flushed a little. "They are speaking very loudly – and I was in the passageway outside for a while."

With her ear to the door, no doubt.

Cassandra shot Jane a look, warning her not to stop their best source of information from sharing what she knew. "How did this all come out?"

"Our Mr Lambton, bless him, went with one of his son's friends to inspect the Canal Company headquarters. An anonymous informant told them something fishy was going on." She wiggled her brows. "And guess what they found?"

"I don't know. What did they find?" Cassandra asked in a suitably awed tone.

"A little notebook saying what she did and how she did it! She's been arrested, they say."

"So," said Jane carefully, "they realize that Mr Gardiner was innocent all along?"

"What?" Mrs Hill cast her a confused look. "Nothing of the sort! Mr Herbert said that she must've been in league with him, you see? She took delivery of the shoddy goods, and they probably were sharing the difference when she turned a blind eye to the quality. He says he's never been so disappointed in anyone in all his life. His own sister!"

That wasn't right. The good-quality damask had been delivered: Reuben had said so. Mr Herbert was placing the blame on his sister, as well as an innocent man, all to make himself sound an innocent dupe of their schemes.

"He thinks she might've been enthralled by the man's charm. She's a widow, vulnerable…" There had seemed nothing vulnerable about Mrs Younge when Jane had met her. "… Such women are often the targets of unscrupulous men," said Mrs Hill sagely.

"Is no one considering that she might be doing this on her own?" asked Cassandra.

"A woman come up with such a scheme?" Mrs Hill clucked her tongue. "Trust me: there will be a man pulling the strings."

Jane was quite convinced that a woman was equally capable of dreaming up such a swindle, but in this case she agreed that there was a man involved, just not the one Mrs Hill had in mind. They were equal partners in this, not a gullible lady led by an unscrupulous gentleman.

"Well, at least there is some good news," continued the landlady. "They caught the wretch. He's under lock and key and won't be getting out again."

"That's a tragedy," muttered Jane.

"Do you think I should serve them some refreshments?" Mrs Hill asked the Austen sisters. "They've been talking in there for a long while."

Jane couldn't care less, but Cassandra nodded politely. "I think that would be appreciated."

"I'd better put out the best linen for them. Governor Harris is there." Mrs Hill went to her linen press and took out a tray cover, unfolding it and smoothing it flat. Little figures on the damask caught Jane's eyes.

"Mrs Hill?" she said hoarsely. "Do you have more of that?"

The landlady held it up. "Pretty, isn't it? Castles – I love castles, especially in a gothic novel like one of Mr Walpole's. I think that's why he gave it to me as a present."

"Who gave it to you?"

"Why, Mr Herbert, of course. He gave me a whole length to make a tablecloth too, instead of his rent one month. I keep that for very best."

"I think this is exactly the right moment for the very best to come out." Jane moved to the closet and found it on the topmost shelf. Her height meant she could reach it easily. She lifted it down.

"Oh, but I was thinking of Christmas and Easter."

"Mrs Hill, if this is what I think it is, it is all my Christmases and Easters rolled into one. Please do me this favour."

Mrs Hill was not a selfish woman; indeed, she lived to please her lodgers, if somewhat haphazardly. "Well, Miss Jane, if it means so much to you."

"I'll lay it out for you, shall I?"

"No need to do that. You're a guest here!"

"There is every need, as you'll soon find out."

With Cassandra at her back and Grandison trotting alongside, Jane headed to the dining room. With a bolstering look at her sister, she opened the door and walked in.

"Jane, Cassandra, this really isn't the place for you to be right now," their father said wearily. Jane could tell he was trying to protect them from the disappointment of finding their evidence being used against the very man they were attempting to clear.

Jane felt attention turn to them and was struck with a momentary dumbness: all those suits and important-looking people, not to mention the scheming look on Mr Herbert's face as he slid his way clear from this fix. Fortunately, Cassandra was undaunted.

"Actually, Papa, we'll only take a moment. Jane?"

Am I an Austen or a mouse? Jane asked herself. Emboldened, she stepped forward and spread the tablecloth out in their midst. It fell with a gratifying elegant flap, like a duchess arranging her train. "Do you recognize this, Mr Herbert?"

He looked at it with horrified recognition and swallowed.

"Mr Governor, Mr Lambton, you see the pattern of the

castles and roses? This was the special commission Mr Gardiner ordered for the Canal Company, the damask that Mr Herbert says was never delivered. If it was never delivered, how did he get hold of it and give it to his landlady in place of his rent?"

Mr Lambton frowned at the Secretary. "I would very much like to know that too." He folded his arms.

"It's a mistake – a misunderstanding – my sister…!" Mr Herbert cast around for excuses but none came up for him. He was beginning to realize that his goose was cooked and decorated with roses.

"You knew Mr Gardiner had sent the good-quality damask and yet you swore in court that he had not," said Governor Harris. "You at the very least have perjured yourself, but I fear your venality goes much deeper. You've benefited from the scheme yourself."

Mr Herbert pressed his lips together.

"Nothing to say?" sneered Henry, looking disgusted by the man. "Well done, Jane!"

Mr Austen stood. "Gentlemen, let's consider what we want to come out of this. We have a man wrongly accused of a crime facing yet more years in prison, or even worse punishment, because he escaped to appeal to us to clear his name. That strikes me as unjust."

The Governor touched the edge of the cloth as if testing that it really was there. It was so white it did have an unearthly appearance to it. "What do you suggest, Austen?"

"Judge Hurst was the trial judge?" Mr Austen steepled his fingers in thought.

"Correct."

"And he is an investor in the canal?"

"Yes, many of us are." The Governor pulled at his cravat somewhat uncomfortably, reminded of the conflict of interest.

"Then I suggest Hurst is approached to consider a pardon and the charges for escape to be dropped. It would be embarrassing if he is discovered to have been duped, and there must be a question of his own monetary matters getting in the way of a fair hearing. If he can be persuaded to recommend a pardon for the man, that will at least secure Gardiner's freedom."

"And what about the guilty ones – Herbert and his sister?"

"I would suggest the law is allowed to take its due course with them."

Mr Herbert scowled at the tablecloth, doubtless wishing he had set fire to it.

Governor Harris considered the proposal, then nodded. "Gentlemen, I'd be obliged if you would escort the prisoner to gaol. I'll send a messenger for Judge Hurst. I think we can get this sorted out swiftly. No one wants confidence in the canal scheme to be knocked in public. A quiet solution, a setting to rights, is preferable, I would say."

Henry and his boat crew marched Mr Herbert out of the room in the wake of the Governor, Mr Lambton, and Mr Austen. As they opened the door, Mrs Hill spilled into the room. She scurried back and gave Governor Harris a curtsey. Everyone ignored the fact that she had been eavesdropping.

Once they were gone, she turned to the girls.

"Well, I never. I always said Mr Herbert had a villainous look!"

Cassandra warned Jane with a press of her hand not to snort. "Indeed, he hasn't shown himself in a good light today."

"Someone should've spent more time reading Fordyce's sermons on good behaviour," said Jane.

Chapter 26

Inspired by their role as gallant knights in the cause of justice, Henry's boat crew went on the next day to triumph over Christchurch College. Henry cemented his reputation among his peers of being a very fine fellow indeed, as well as being a hero to his sisters for standing by them in their defence of Gardiner.

Once more spectating at the boathouses, Jane gave him a hug and a kiss as he decorated her head with the crown of bay leaves that he had been sporting. "You will be my favourite brother for a little longer," she promised him.

"And you my joint-favourite sister for all time!" He picked her up and swung her in a circle.

Jane laughed. That was exactly how it should be.

They left Henry to his celebrations to head back to Mrs Hill's to pack up their belongings. The chaise had been ordered and their mother told to expect them the following day.

"Before we start for home, my dears," said Mr Austen, "there is someone who wants to meet you." He steered them on a little detour to the prison. "I think you can guess who that might be?"

Jane nodded, emotion clogging her throat.

"You can't tell anyone about this, of course. No mention in letters or conversation," he continued.

"Of course," said Cassandra, speaking for them both.

They passed through the gateway as far as the Governor's house. This was not in the main courtyard but set a little apart as befitting a gentleman's residence. A maid opened the door and showed them into a sunny parlour.

Gardiner was sitting on an upright chair by the fire. His appearance was much improved now he had had a chance to bathe and shave. Gone was the fearsome bear of a man, in his place a gentle but battered giant. He got up as soon as he saw them, fumbling the brim of his hat that he held in nervous fingers.

Governor Harris came in from his study, which lay just beyond the parlour.

"Miss Austen, Miss Jane, here is a man who is most anxious to meet you." Harris beamed at them. "He knows that it is primarily thanks to your recognition of the damask tablecloth that his innocence was proven yesterday." The Governor turned to their father. "They must be accomplished needleworkers to have such a good eye for material. Girls a father can be proud of!"

Not to mention their investigative skills, thought Jane, but she knew her father had gone out of his way to keep their names out of the discovery of the accounts book. She wasn't about to jeopardize that.

"Ladies, I'm much obliged to you," Gardiner said gruffly. His shrewd look at Jane told her he for one knew they had done more than notice a pattern on a piece of cloth.

"It was our pleasure – and our duty," said Cassandra.

"I am in your debt."

"You owe us nothing – unless it be to live happily ever after," said Jane.

He smiled wryly. "I'll try, but I have only secured a pardon, and not cleared my name. Reopening my case was judged too difficult, as I am judged guilty of breaking out of gaol."

"That seems so unfair!" Jane took a seat near him.

He sat back down and rested his big hands on his knees. "Such is life, young lady. I have compromised and accepted that freedom is the best I can ask for. I'll now have to start over somewhere else."

"I hope you will remember Mr Reuben if you do," said Cassandra. "He was your staunchest defender."

He gave a sad smile. "If ever I am in the position to offer him work, I will write at once. He's a good man."

"The Canal Company have offered you compensation, don't forget," said Harris. "Enough to start a new business."

"Aye, they have. Perhaps it is for the best," said Gardiner, looking away wistfully. "Everyone here will remember, suspicion will always hang over me. I'll go to my family in Coventry, if I can slip away unremarked. I've had enough of public notoriety."

Jane clasped her hands to her chest as a wonderful idea bloomed. "Oh, Mr Gardiner, I think we can help with that too! What do you think about taking a canal trip?"

He pulled a face. "I'd be happy never to see a speck of canal mud again."

She hadn't thought of that. To him, the canal meant servitude, whereas to her it meant freedom. "But this is different, the people quite delightful, and they have no prejudice against you. In fact, they would be proud to let you travel with them."

A slow smile broke over his face, some of the old Mr Gardiner, before all his sorrow, coming back. "In that case, Miss Jane, lead on."

Jane, Cassandra, and Mr Austen watched as Gardiner led Nettlebed along the towpath. The free man waved and smiled, before facing forwards and finding a steady pace to match the horse's. The prospect of walking for miles in an unhurried manner, not having to fear for his liberty and life, was a soothing balm for him, he had said. The Carters had been swift to agree to carry the passenger with them, and Rag-N'-Bone had concurred with Grandison that Gardiner was a dog-friendly person, so his welcome onboard was assured.

The Austens had said their farewells and paused only to watch the narrowboat slide away into the misty autumn day before they too set out on their journey, though they would be snug in their chaise for Steventon. On the boat, Georgie stood at the stern, hand on the tiller, chewing on a grass stalk with her hat pushed back, at ease with her roving life. Jane felt once more, and for a final time, the pang of desire that she too could go with them, threading her way through the silver veins of canals connecting the entire kingdom. What a life that would be!

But no, her place was with the people beside her. Her family, her village, her home.

Grandison nudged her hand and she rested it on his head, rubbing his ear thoughtfully.

"Well, I have to say, my dears," said Mr Austen, "that wasn't the visit to Oxford I expected."

"Nor I. I'll never look at a draper's shop in the same way again," said Cassandra. "And I'll certainly pay much more attention to the quality of the cloth I buy."

Jane smiled at her sister's practical lesson drawn from events.

"And what about you, Jane?" asked Mr Austen, offering his arms to escort his daughters to the carriage.

Jane took his arm. "I've learned not to trust my first impressions – and to consider investing in canals. They are quite the coming thing, don't you know?"

Her father and Cassandra laughed.

"Put your purse away, Jane," said her father. "I don't want any more talk of canals in our household. It's time I took you both home."